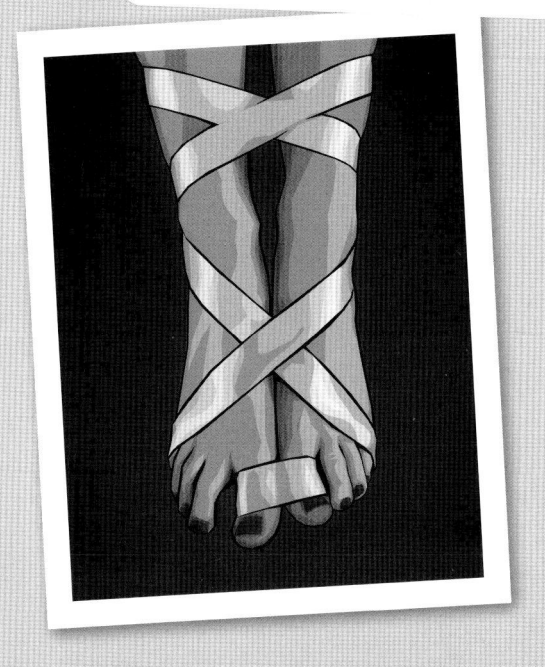

50 Nights in Gray
A Sensual Journey in Black and White

50 Nights in Gray
A Sensual Journey in Black and White

Text **Laura Elias**
Illustrations **Benjamin Wachenje**

weldon**owen**

CONTENTS

NIGHT ONE The Journey Begins
NIGHT TWO Lust on Ice
NIGHT THREE Desire Takes Flight
NIGHT FOUR The Slow Strip
NIGHT FIVE Coming Clean
NIGHT SIX Through the Lens
NIGHT SEVEN In the Public Eye
NIGHT EIGHT After Hours
NIGHT NINE The Heat of the Moment
NIGHT TEN The Naughty Missionary
NIGHT ELEVEN From the Waist Up
NIGHT TWELVE Eat Me Up

NIGHT THIRTEEN	Head Over Heels
NIGHT FOURTEEN	A Touch of the Lash
NIGHT FIFTEEN	Bad Girls Get Spanked
NIGHT SIXTEEN	Taken from Behind
NIGHT SEVENTEEN	At Your Service
NIGHT EIGHTEEN	Deep Love
NIGHT NINETEEN	Helpless with Pleasure
NIGHT TWENTY	Swept Off My Feet
NIGHT TWENTY-ONE	A Firm Hand
NIGHT TWENTY-TWO	Pain Becomes Pleasure
NIGHT TWENTY-THREE	You Will Meet a Stranger
NIGHT TWENTY-FOUR	The Rule of Three
NIGHT TWENTY-FIVE	The Girl in the Long Red Coat

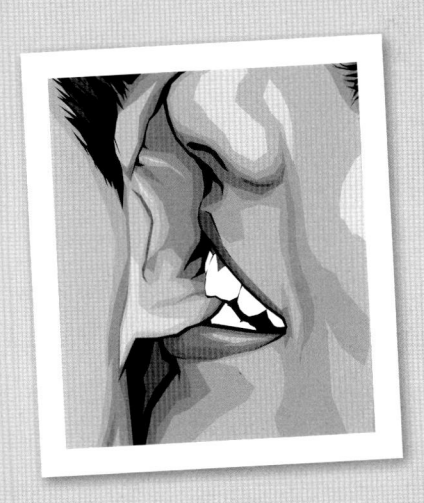

NIGHT TWENTY-SIX	The Changing of the Guard
NIGHT TWENTY-SEVEN	A Foretaste of Pleasure
NIGHT TWENTY-EIGHT	Story Hour
NIGHT TWENTY-NINE	Trust Me
NIGHT THIRTY	Taking the Collar
NIGHT THIRTY-ONE	In My Hands
NIGHT THIRTY-TWO	Caught in the Middle
NIGHT THIRTY-THREE	Taking Your Licks
NIGHT THIRTY-FOUR	Teacher Needs to See You After School
NIGHT THIRTY-FIVE	I'll Be Watching You
NIGHT THIRTY-SIX	I Toe the Line
NIGHT THIRTY-SEVEN	The Stiletto Samba
NIGHT THIRTY-EIGHT	Kitten in Heels
NIGHT THIRTY-NINE	The Wake-Up Call
NIGHT FORTY	X Marks the Spot
NIGHT FORTY-ONE	In a Bind
NIGHT FORTY-TWO	Traffic Stop
NIGHT FORTY-THREE	Stay a While
NIGHT FORTY-FOUR	Behind My Man
NIGHT FORTY-FIVE	The Back Passage
NIGHT FORTY-SIX	The Journey Continues
NIGHT FORTY-SEVEN	Face to Face
NIGHT FORTY-EIGHT	A Tantalizing Toybag
NIGHT FORTY-NINE	Going Up
NIGHT FIFTY	Closing the Book

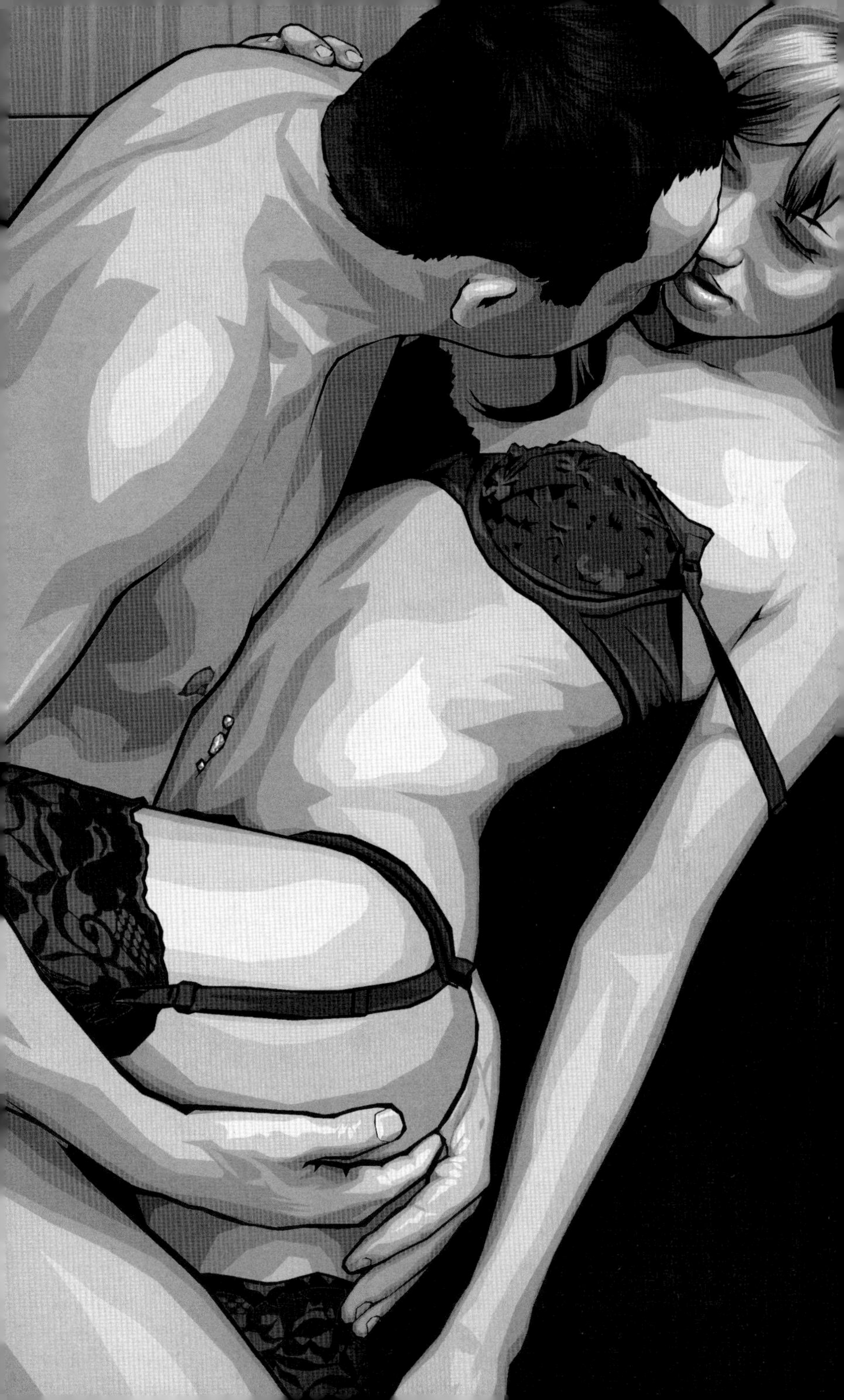

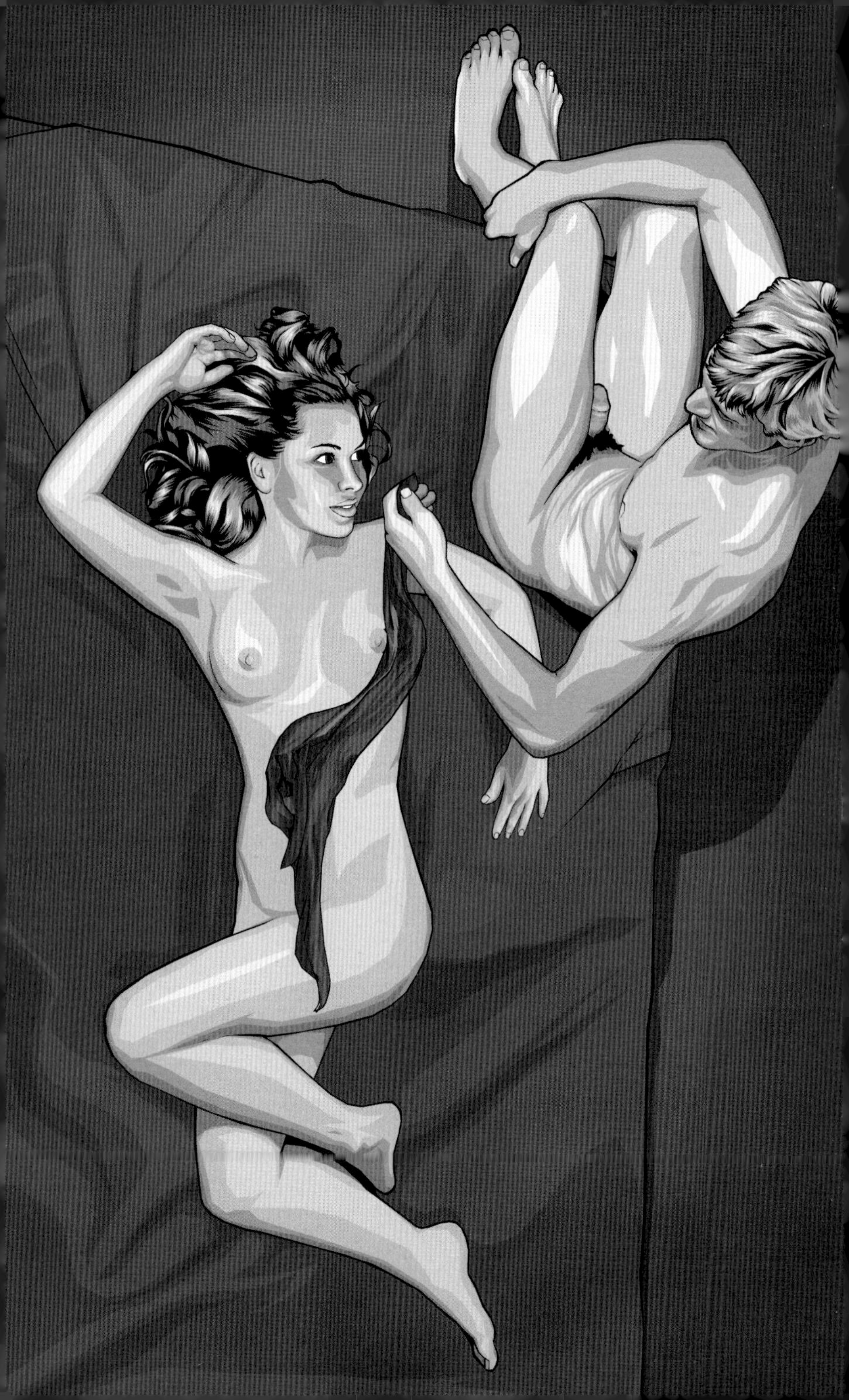

NIGHT ONE
The Journey Begins

"I want to learn," I told him, as I lay back on the bed, still a little dazed from the intensity of our lovemaking. He trailed a silk scarf down my body, sending little ripples of sensation along my skin. "There's a lot to learn," he said. "What do you want to know?"

"Everything," I said bravely, after a brief hesitation. Did I really want to open this door? Could I even guess what might lie behind it? "Everything," I repeated, a bit more firmly.

He smiled. "Then your education begins tomorrow. When you wake, I will have delivered a blank journal to you. I want you to document your journey, your investigations, the lessons we will study together. Show your work—this is a serious assignment. I want to see pictures, instructions, and, above all, your personal reflections. The results may ... surprise you."

"Will I be graded?" I joked. He looked silently at me, and suddenly I felt a little nervous. What had I just signed up for?

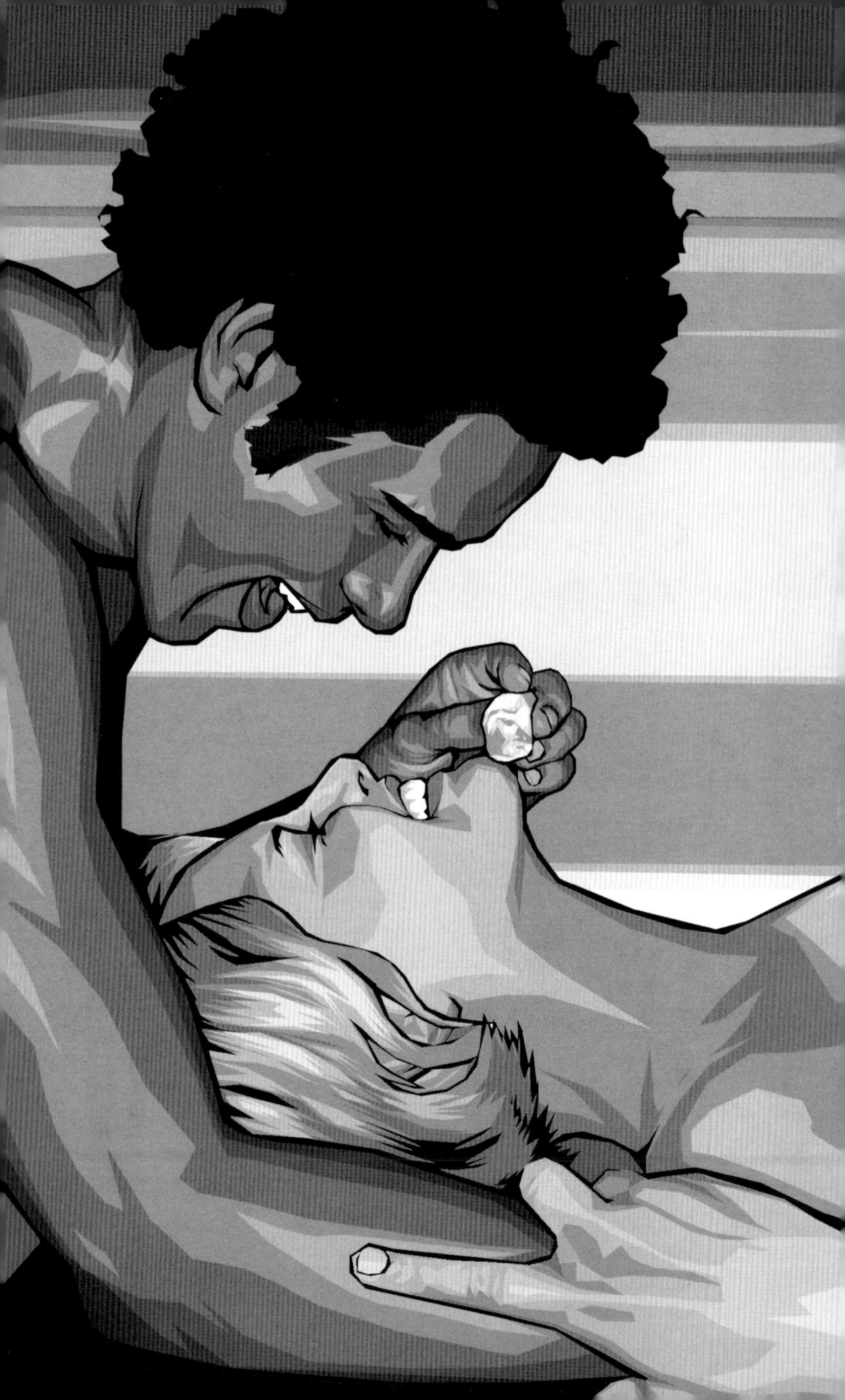

Night Two
Lust on Ice

"Where are we going?" I whispered, gazing out of the cockpit of his private jet. "You'll find out soon enough," he said, as he shifted the yoke.

Dry canyons and golden sands appeared below, and the sun's merciless heat pressed in around us as we landed. "Undress," he ordered. I gasped. Was he ordering me to walk naked into a searing desert?

The heat hit me like a wall of flame as I walked barefoot down the plane's steps. "Come," he commanded, leading me to a white silken tent. "Lie down." I stretched out on satin sheets, my body slicked with sweat.

Our lips met as he leaned over me; his kiss was glacial, and I jolted at the icy chill. "Down," he said, and took an ice cube from his mouth, drawing it over my burning skin. The contrast was startling . . . and intensely erotic.

He swept the melting ice across my nipples, making them stiffen, then tugged them with hot fingertips, and I moaned at the sudden change. "You're very hot, darling," he said, circling the ice around my navel, and down. "Let's see if we can cool you off." I parted my legs, awaiting his icy touch on my innermost need.

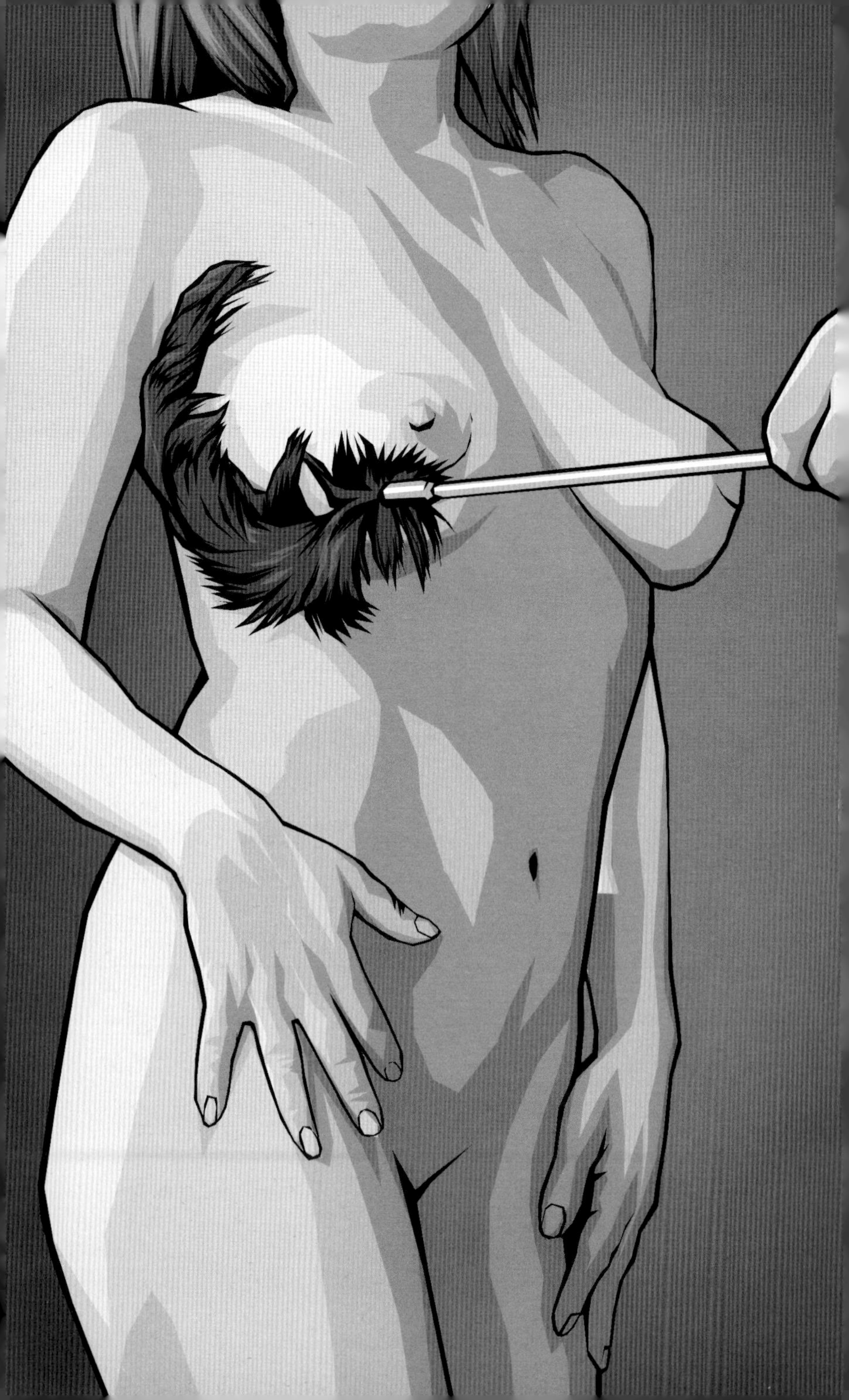

Night Three
Desire Takes Flight

    The next evening, he undressed me in front of his living room windows. As the city glimmered below, he slid the straps of my dress off my shoulders, then deftly unclasped my bra and pushed down my panties.

    "Remain still," he said, and slid open the glass doors to the balcony. Cool night air teased me, increasing my anticipation as he reached into an antique bureau. "Close your eyes," he ordered, and I quickly obeyed. Something soft and ticklish curved across my breasts, and I arched my back, maddened by the gentle teasing. "More," I whispered, surprising myself.

    "Quiet," he hissed, drawing the soft object over my shoulders, and up to my lips. Finally he drew it downward and flicked it mockingly across my nipples. I moaned as he traced small circles down my abdomen.

    He parted my thighs with his hands, and curiosity got the better of me. I peeked, and saw that he held a long crimson feather, which he drew slowly between my thighs. I opened my legs wider, shaking with the sensation as he gently teased me. "Touch me now," I begged.

    "Later," he said, smiling. "There's so much more I'll do to you first, my darling."

THE SEXY SECRET

1. Ask your partner which outfit you should wear for his pleasure. Pin up your hair so you can later shake it down as you strip. Be sure to avoid anything too complicated.

2. Caress your body with your hands so he can imagine what's under those clothes. Tell him he can't touch you until you say so.

3. If you're stripping out of a skirt, don't shatter the fantasy by tripping over it. Pin it down with one foot while freeing the other, then kick it away.

4. Turn, pose, cock a hip, and toss your hair in loose, sexy tendrils as you remove each piece of clothing.

5. Those sexy shoes come off last—if at all. There's nothing like a pair of pumps on a beautiful, naked woman. Stockings too? Your call. Experiment to see what works.

NIGHT FOUR
The Slow Strip

"You're learning," he said to me, turning the pages of my journal. "But you're still only a student. I've been seducing you, but now it's time for you to seduce me."

"How can I do that?" He'd always been the one to say what he wanted, always the one to taunt and tease—never the other way around.

"Stand up," he commanded. I did, nervously smoothing the simple blouse and skirt I'd worn to work that day. "Good," he said. "Run your hands over your body. You're going to strip for me."

He touched a button, and sensual music filled the room. I blushed, but slid my hands down my sides, unbuttoned my blouse, and let it drape off my shoulders.

"Very good," he said. I let the blouse fall, growing more confident, reaching for the waist of my skirt. He stopped me with a look. "Slowly." I nudged the blouse away with a heel and raised the skirt to flash my garters. He hissed out a breath, and I turned, teasing him with a rear view. "Now," he said. I slid slowly out of the skirt.

I stood before him in the heels and lingerie he'd bought for me, and felt suddenly powerful. I began to ease my panties over my hips as he reached for me ...

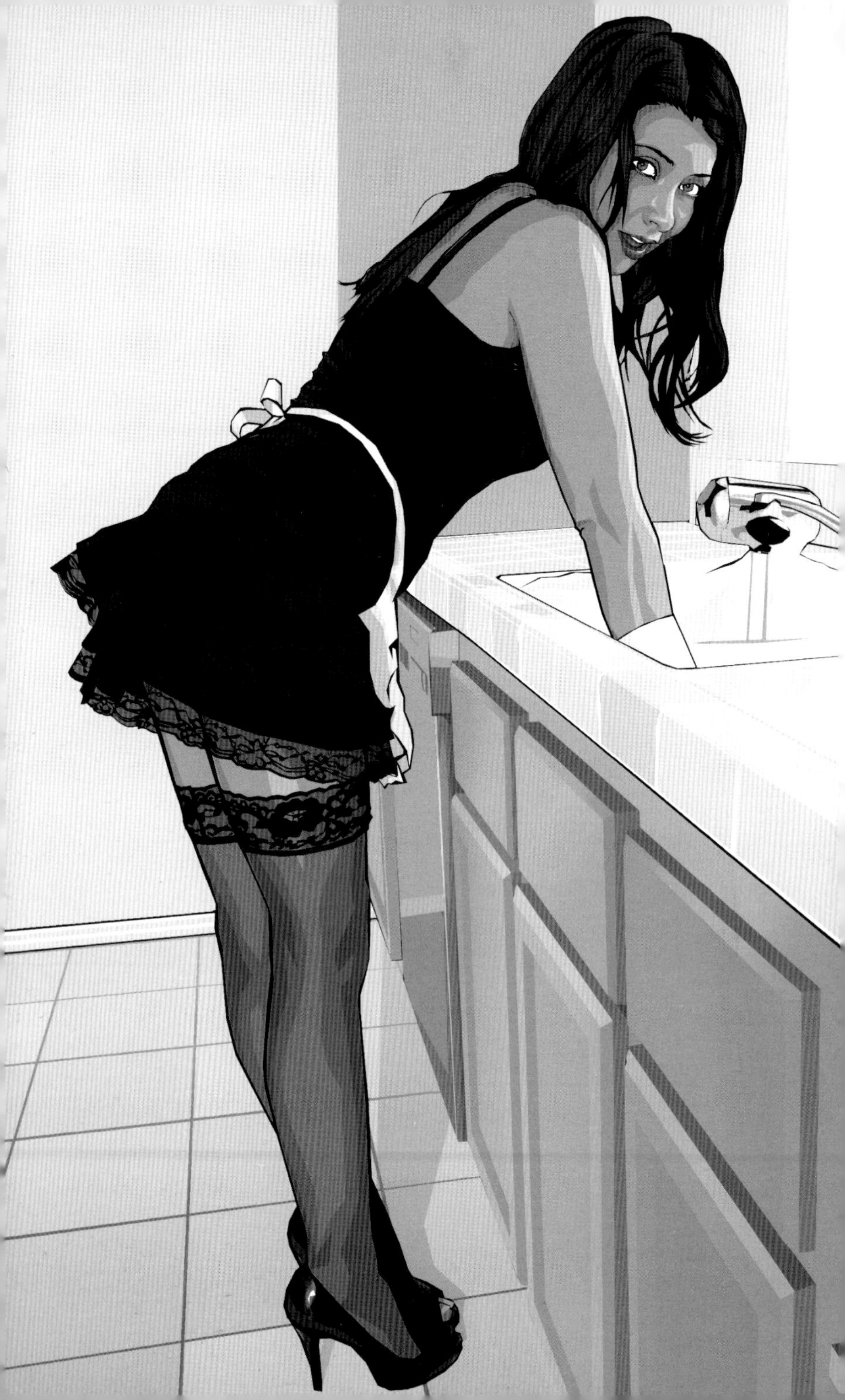

NIGHT FIVE
Coming Clean

The sun was setting when I arrived at the hotel. I had a surprise for him—and I couldn't wait to show it off. I laid out the things I'd bought: a short black dress, a tiny white-lace apron, black stockings, black pumps... and a pair of thin latex gloves. Perfect for washing the dishes, I thought as I dressed—or a sexy man.

It seemed crazy—maybe he'd laugh, or get angry. But I felt like someone else in those scraps of lace and silk. When I heard his key in the door, I went into the bathroom, turned on the faucet, and plunged my gloved hands into the sink. He halted at the doorway, watching while I arched my back to show a glimpse of my rear under the tiny skirt. I sank to my knees, running the sponge over the pristine tiles, making sure he could see my breasts rising and falling.

"You missed a spot," he said softly as he knelt behind me and took hold of my hands, slowly stripping off the gloves. "And maids who can't do their jobs properly..." My head fell back upon his shoulder as he used my own hands to caress me through the uniform, whispering all the delicious punishments to come.

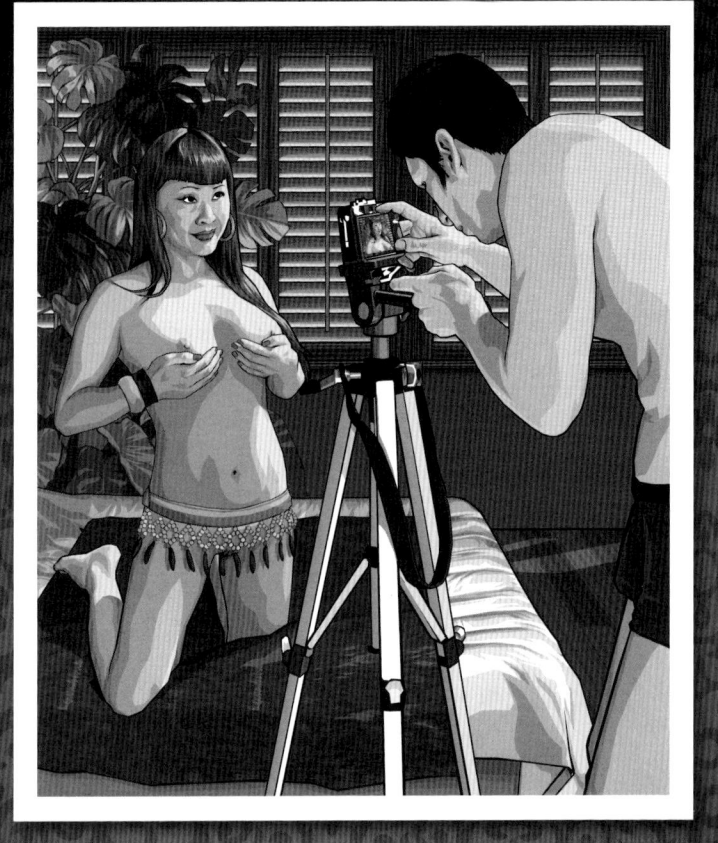

THE SEXY SECRET

1. Create a sensual setting. Choose rich fabrics and costumes for an opulent look, or clear away clutter for simple photographs that emphasize the naked body.

2. Work without a flash, which can cast harsh and unflattering light. Use diffused, natural light from a window (angling your lover's profile against this light brings out a curvy silhouette) or, for a professional set-up, use a studio strobe and a soft box.

3. Explore your lover's body from near and far. Capture his or her entire frame, then zoom in on legs, hands, or feet, looking for beauty in unexpected places such as the slope of a hip.

4. Leave the traditionally sexy parts—breasts, buttocks, genitals—for last, when your partner is relaxed. Afterward, set down your camera for a 3-D appreciation of your lover's body, or switch places and let your lover photograph you.

NIGHT SIX
Through the Lens

After hours of lovemaking, the light of dawn shone through the curtains. I rose to shower, but he pinned me back down. "Tell me your dreams," he ordered.

I laughed. "You didn't leave time for dreams."

"Then tell me what you'd like to dream. Who you'd be. What you'd do." School was back in session.

"I dream," I began, tentatively, "that you're a stranger. You hire me to visit you in some tropical town." He nodded, sitting up. "I don't know what you want from me. But I come into the room, and see..."

"What do you see?" He asked, listening intently.

"Cameras. Old ones and new, all around the room."

He stirred, intrigued, and I continued. "You tell me to undress, as you set up a camera on a tripod."

"What do I do with you? Tell me," he urged.

"You give me jewelry to wear. Then you pull me to my knees on the bed. I offer my breasts to your lens"—he took my nipple in his lips as I spoke—"and I caress myself. I do everything I can to lure you out from behind the camera."

"Do you succeed?" he murmured.

"The dream ends there," I said, embracing him.

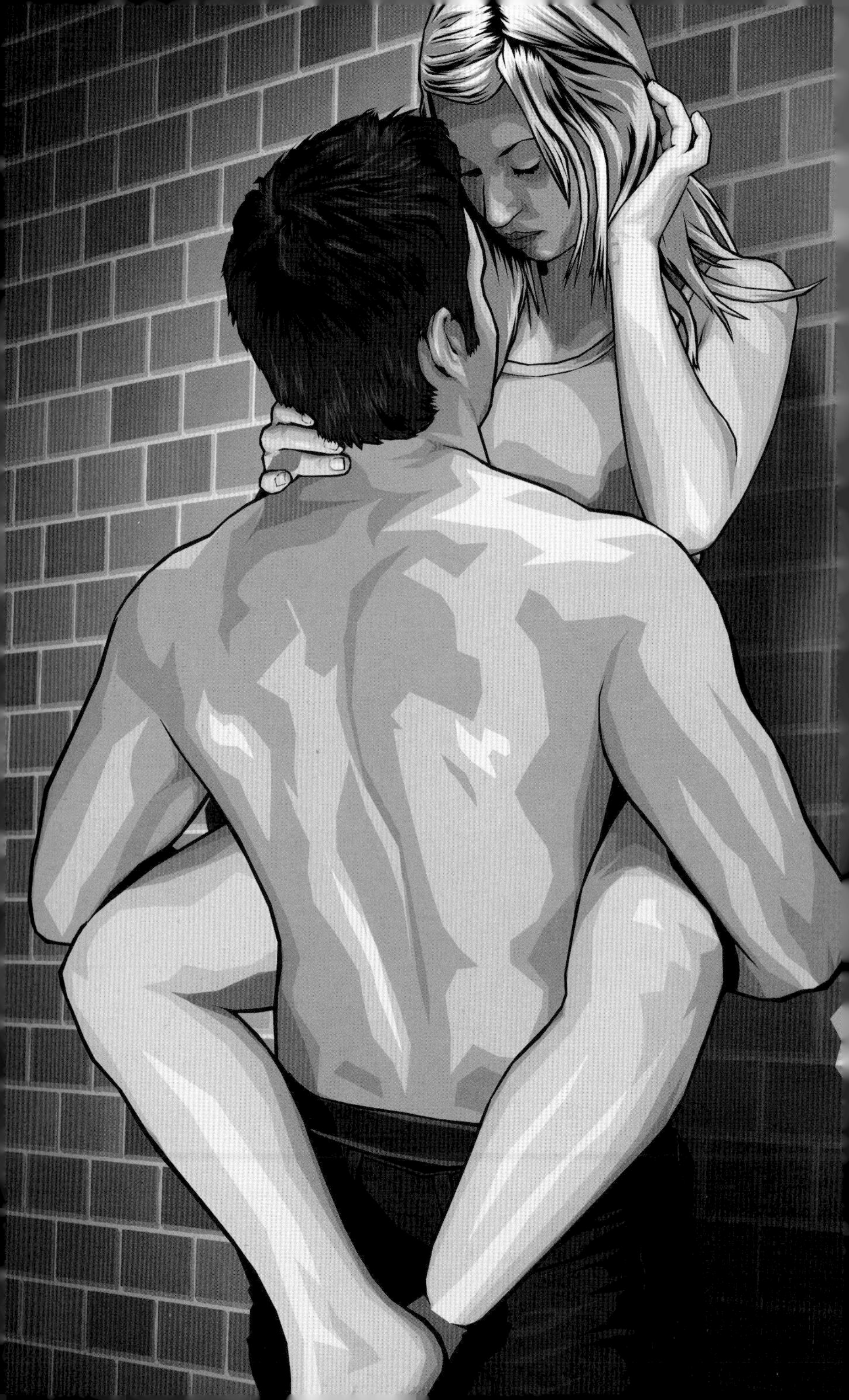

Night Seven
In the Public Eye

"Let's go to the movies tonight," he said on the phone. The movies... was that all? I felt disappointed, like a teenager facing a boring date. But I agreed.

I shifted uncomfortably in my seat through the opening credits of a mainstream romantic comedy. He likes this stuff? I looked at his profile in the dark, and he turned to me, smiling. Then, he silently pulled me from my seat, heading to the exit.

"So you were bored, too," I teased him.

He pushed me to the wall of the alley. "I'm never bored when I'm imagining what I will do with you."

Even the bricks felt hot in the summer night as he lifted my skirt with one hand, winding one of my legs around his waist. "I have another instruction for you. When we're out together, you will never wear underwear. I want access to you whenever, and wherever, I wish."

"Yes, sir," I smiled into his collarbone. He yanked my panties down until they ripped, then lifted me up. As he entered me, I heard voices at the mouth of the alley, the laughter of young men and women.

"They'll see us," I breathed.

"Let them see us," he told me. "Let them see it all."

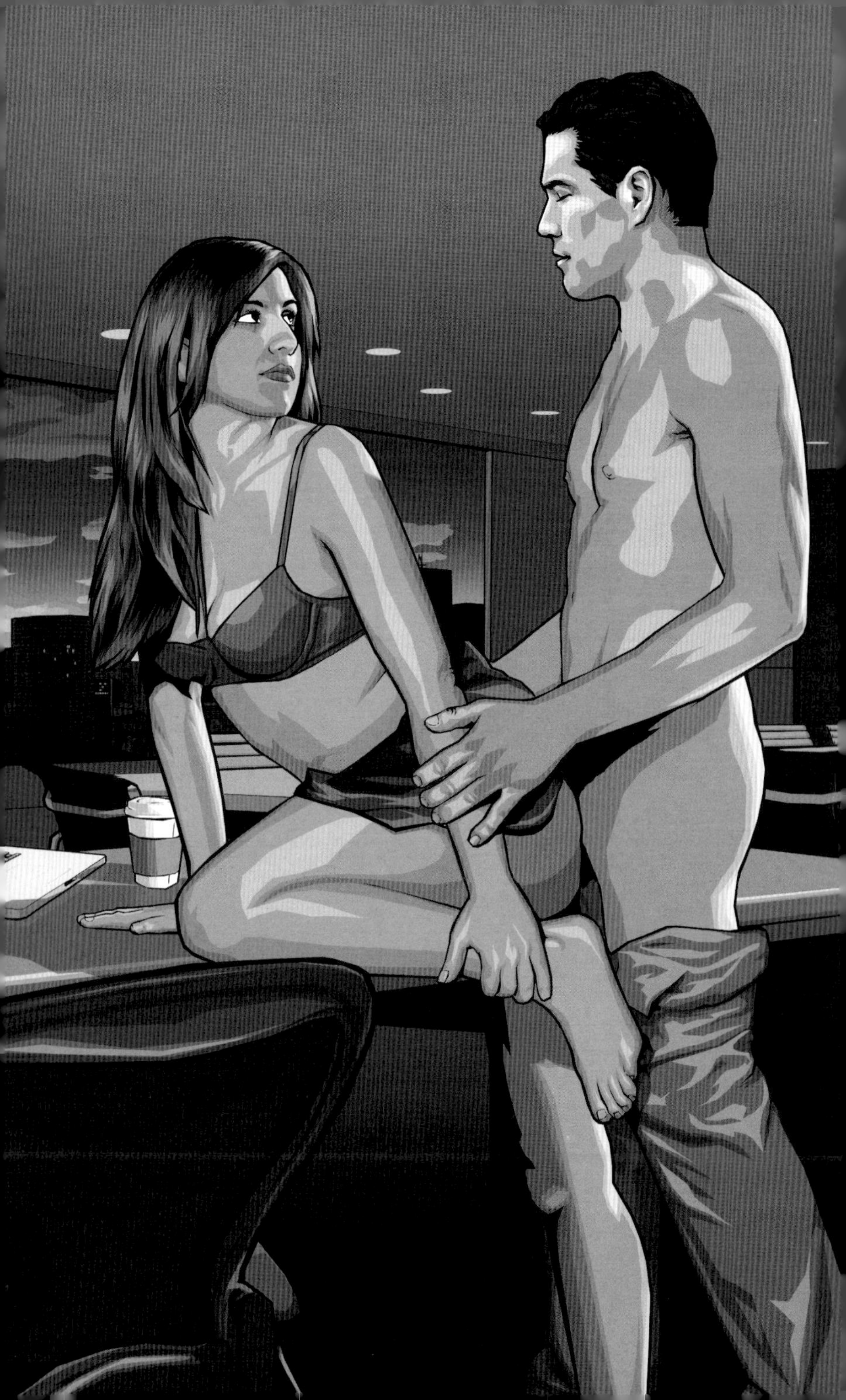

NIGHT EIGHT
After Hours

No time for him tonight, I thought, forcing my eyes back to the numbers on the screen. There'd be hell to pay if I didn't get these figures done by morning. I silenced my phone and tried to shut out all thoughts of him. Friday night was for dates, dinner, dancing—yet here I sat.

I sighed, rubbing my eyes with both hands. "You look weary, my love," said a voice. There he was, stern and tall in his dark suit. He set an espresso before me. "Drink. You'll need the energy."

"How did you get in the building?" I asked, sipping obediently. He smiled, then leaned over and turned my computer to sleep mode. "Hey! I'm not finished!" I was genuinely peeved. "What do you think you're doing?"

"Let me show you, darling," he said, drawing me from my chair, working his hands over my taut shoulders. I sighed, succumbing to his touch as he lifted my shirt to caress my skin. Work or not, I could never resist him.

I bent forward across the desk, giving in. The whisper of fabric told me he was disrobing. "Arch your back for me. Yes, like that." I turned my head to see his face, quiet, intent, eyes closed, body working. Working for me. I smiled. The budget could wait.

THE SEXY SECRET:

1. Lay down a sheet or towel that you don't mind throwing away after, to protect bedclothes.

2. Use a special massage candle or a plain, unscented white paraffin candles (dyes can burn).

3. Let wax pool in the candle before dripping, to cool it a bit. Test it on the inside of your wrist to make sure its cool enough before using on your partner.

4. Start dripping from at least three feet above your partner; if they enjoy the sensation, try dripping from a lower height to intensify sensation.

5. A massage candle's wax turns to scented oil. With a regular candle, you'll need to carefully scrape the wax off with a butter knife.

NIGHT NINE
The Heat of the Moment

When he led me into the bedroom, I thought it seemed... uncharacteristically romantic.

The bed was draped in satin; a row of simple white candles flickered on the table. Had my prince of pain decided on a more conventional evening, with satin sheets and soft candlelight? "Lie down," he instructed me, pushing me to the bed, my face smothered in the folds of satin. Naked, exposed, I shivered in the cool night air.

"Perhaps this might warm you up," he whispered, and I felt something splash onto my skin. The sensation was repeated, first warm and sensual, then sharper, hotter, almost scalding. The candles! He was dripping wax onto my skin, raising and lowering the candle to vary the intensity, and my pleasure.

All too soon, I felt cold steel against my skin. I tensed nervously, but he was only using the flat of a knife to scrape the wax from my skin, teasing me with the blade. When my skin was clean, he sank his strong fingers into my flesh, kneading away my tension, preparing me for what would come next.

Night Ten
The Naughty Missionary

"Onto the bed," he whispered to me. We were fresh from the shower and I'd been expecting something... unusual. He'd teased and tasted me under the spray until I was desperate to have him inside me.

Not desperate enough, it seemed. I hesitated a moment, enjoying the anticipation, and the sight of his all-too-obvious excitement. "I said, onto the bed," he growled, pushing me so that I half-stumbled, falling backwards. "That's better," he said, roughly spreading my legs. And in a moment he had entered me, fast and hard, knowing that our sensual shower had been more than enough foreplay.

He felt good inside me, better than good, but I was surprised that he wanted only this simplest of positions. Were we back to square one? "Is this all you have for me tonight?" I whispered mockingly.

That did it. He was on his knees in a flash, grabbing my ankles and crossing them before his chest. I couldn't move my legs as he pressed deeper inside me, the pressure near-painful as I tightened around him. "That's what I have tonight for sassy girls," he whispered, barely moving, rubbing the base of his erection with slow, unbearable delight across my clitoris.

He gripped my ankles tighter as I tried to pull away, never breaking eye contact. "Don't struggle, love," he said. "You're under my control." I pressed at his strong thighs with my palms, trying to slow the growing heat inside me. "Lie back. Hands over your head." I obeyed, and he rocked more slowly still as my body tensed, building toward the tumultuous ending we could both sense approaching like a distant storm ...

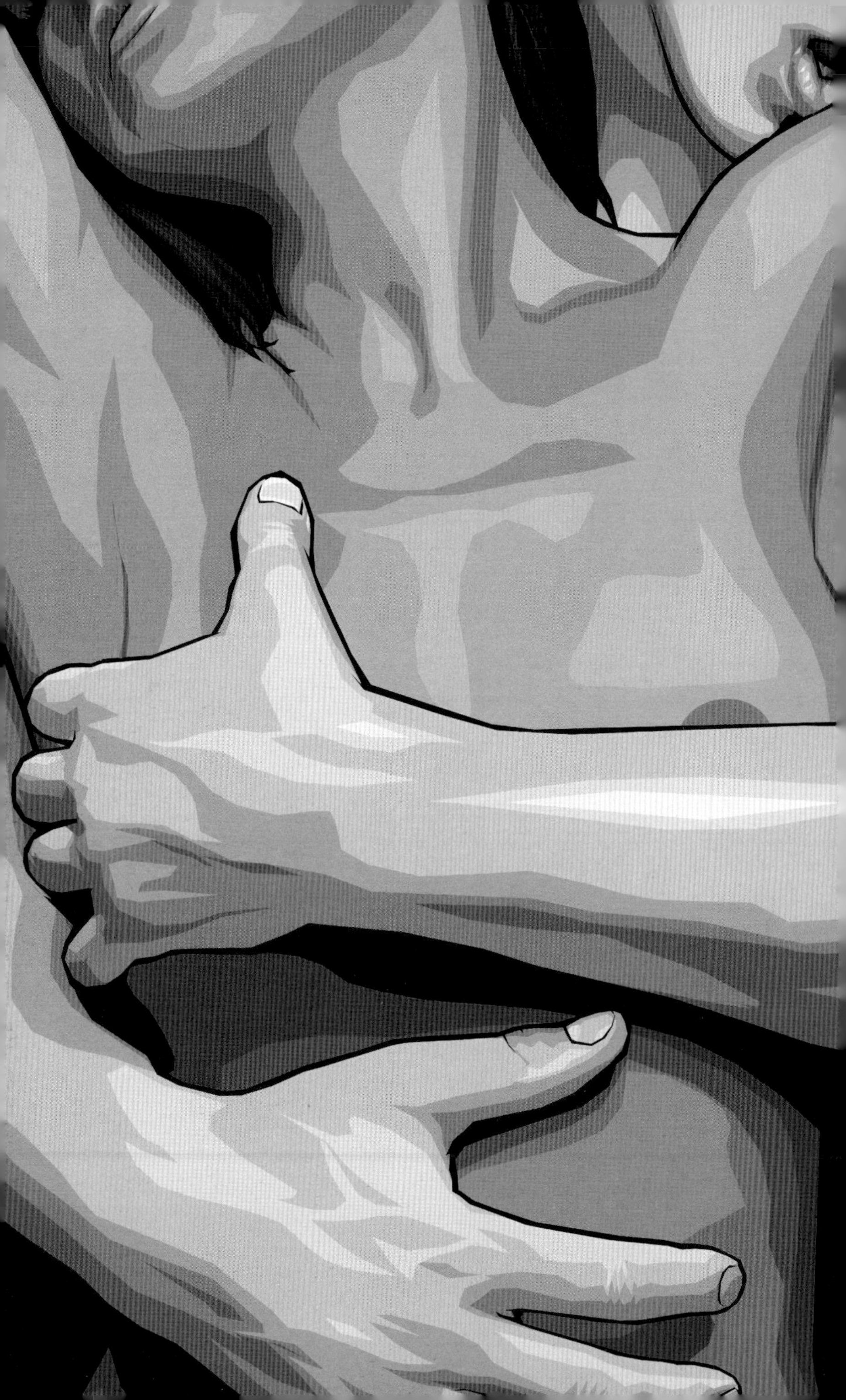

Night Eleven
From the Waist Up

In his playroom that night—the secret room with its beguiling toys and tools—he set out a simple mahogany chair. I began to ask what he intended, and he placed his hand over my mouth. "One lesson you must learn, my dear," he began, "is to speak only when spoken to."

I glanced up at him as he sat me down, and he smiled teasingly. "Tonight we test your ... responsiveness." He poured scented oil into his hands, stroking around my breasts, down my stomach. I spread my thighs, but he ignored me, cupping my breasts as if judging their weight. I gasped as he gently flicked his oiled fingers across my nipples. He bent down, nibbling each one in turn, and I pushed his hands lower, lower. "Oh, no, you don't," he said, taking my arms. I felt the brush of silken cord as he bound my wrists behind me.

My back arched as he bit and stroked, his lips and fingers moving deftly. Electricity flowed from my nipples to my core and back again. Then he closed his teeth sharply on one nipple, pulling hard on the other, and I threw my head back, crying out as I reached orgasm.

"Very good," he praised. "You've passed the test—this one, at least."

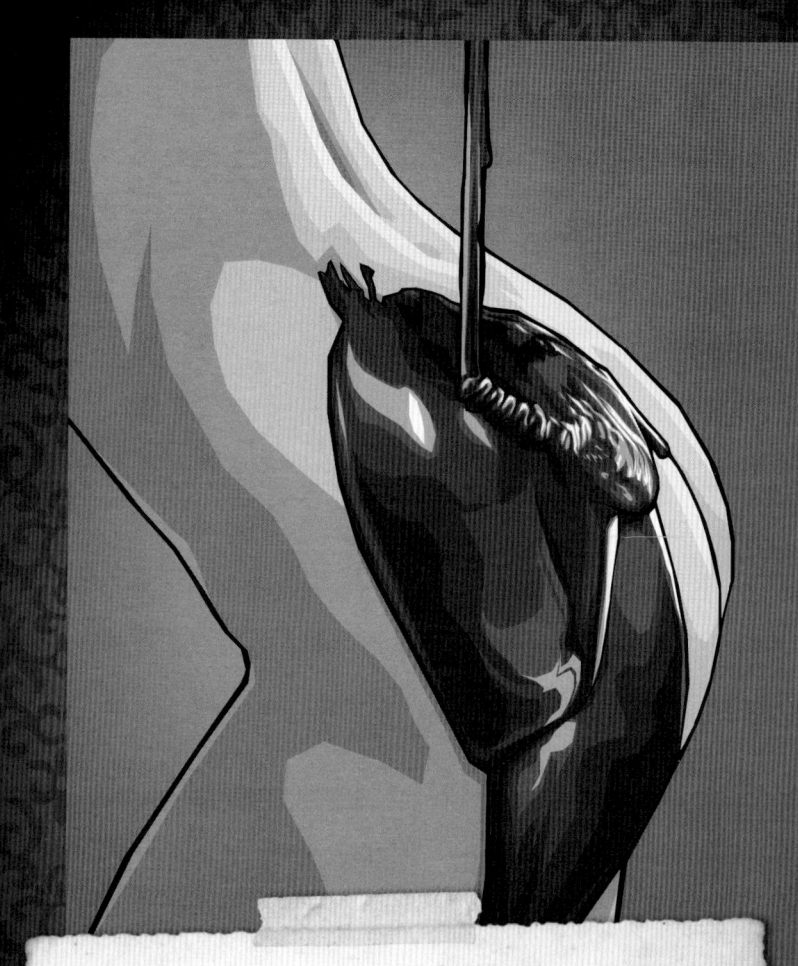

THE SEXY SECRET:

1. Some foods—oysters, asparagus—enjoy a rep as aphrodisiacs, but anything edible can spice up sex. Food provokes many senses (taste, smell, touch), so it naturally enhances your experience. Play in the kitchen or lay down a tablecloth for easy clean-up.

2. Classics such as whipped cream and chocolate turn breasts and penises into tasty lick-it-up treats, but sample other foods too. Pass a slice of ripe mango from mouth to mouth. Lick soft cheese or pudding off each other's fingers. Sip liqueur from her navel. But don't take yourselves too seriously. This is playtime.

3. Keep foods out of the vagina and anus—they can cause irritation or infection—or put a lubed condom over vegetables and fruits that you'll insert.

Night Twelve
Eat Me Up

At the bookstore, he perused a thick biography while I drifted toward the cooking section. *A Thousand Dessert Dreams*, one title read. Tempting photos of mousses, fondants, cakes, and bonbons flashed by as I flipped through its pages, an idea growing in my mind.

"And what are you reading?" he breathed into my ear. No one was around; he ran a finger along the hem of my skirt, teasing my thigh. I pushed back against him.

"Thinking about your... dessert," I said, shifting my hips until I could feel his growing erection. "We'll start in the kitchen. Nothing on me but an apron. We'll need, uh—" I paused as his hand slipped between my legs, "a saucepan of warm melted chocolate. And a big spoon."

"What then, my darling?"

"You lean me over the counter," I said, and his fingers entered me sharply. "You use the spoon to drizzle the chocolate down my back. It's hot, and I gasp."

"I rub the chocolate all over your creamy ass," he said. I heard his zipper, and he leaned me forward, entering me in one motion. "I lick it off, rub my fingers in it, and give you a taste." Oh, he was delicious. "And when you're all clean, I start again. Caramel, this time."

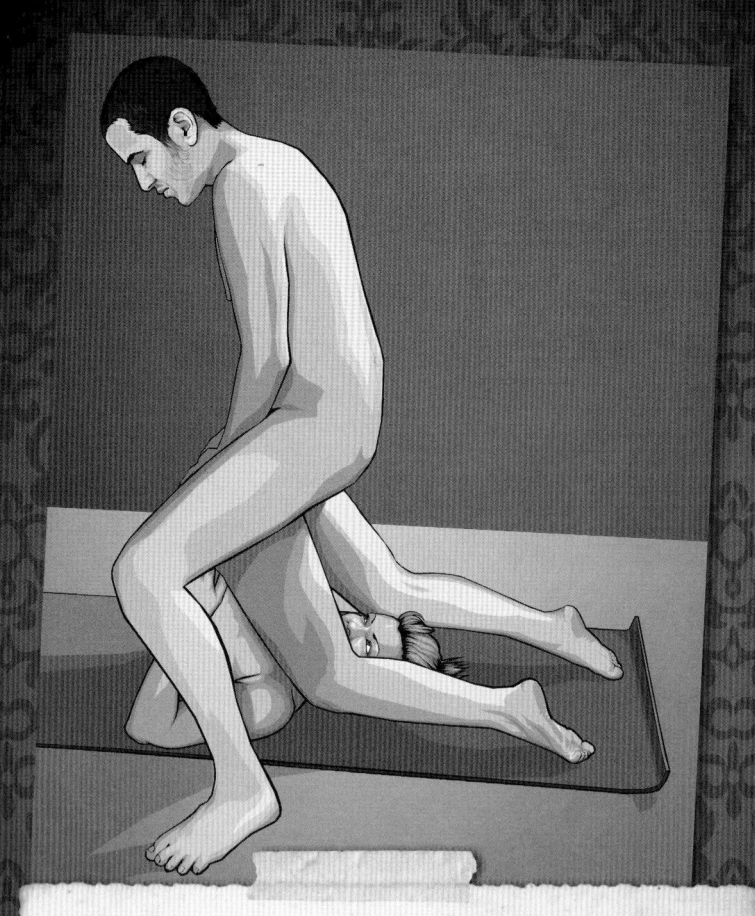

THE SEXY SECRET:

1. The woman needs to be limber for this position, no question, but you can help out by bracing the back and shoulders against a piece of furniture, and support her hips with her hands or a pillow as her partner thrusts downward. Don't exert pressure on the woman's flexed neck. This is also quite a workout for the man, as he's supporting his weight and thrusting from an unusual angle.

2. Change it up: This position works equally well for vaginal and anal sex, and the man can turn around so he's facing the woman's feet and enter her again, stimulating her from a new angle.

3. Try a variation: If the yoga position is too challenging, the woman can try a modified doggie-style position with her rear elevated to allow for deep penetration from the same angle.

Night Thirteen
Head Over Heels

Some evenings after work, I sneaked into his gym to watch him exercise. I relaxed in the hallway, while behind plate-glass windows he lifted weights at his trainer's command, or stretched into various positions as she told him to shift that leg, extend that arm. He was beautiful; I loved seeing him under someone else's control.

One night he saw me through the window, and a black cloud crossed his features. I knew punishment would follow. He grabbed his towel, left the weight room, and pulled me out of the gym by my wrist. He drove us home without a word and pushed me into the playroom. "So you like to see me follow orders," he said.

Still damp with sweat, he removed his shorts and spread a mat on the floor. "My workout isn't done yet," he said, stripping me quickly.

"Plow position," he commanded, and barely gave me time to react. He pushed me onto my back and swept my ankles over my head, exposing me beneath him. He aimed his erection down and into me, his thighs flexing. Oh, my god, I thought. He waited a moment, then pulled slowly upward and down again, stretching and opening me for his own pleasure as I lay helpless below him.

THE SEXY SECRET:

1. Floggers—available at most sex shops or from online retailers—can be made of many materials. If you're a novice, start with something soft, like satin ribbons.

2. Start slowly, trailing the flogger's lashes gently over your partner's body. Next, see how a light strike of the flogger feels on her back and buttocks. Nice? Try a slightly firmer strike. Aim for fleshy areas, not bony ones.

3. After you and your partner are experienced floggers, sample new materials. Rubber can be very stimulating to some; others prefer classic leather or floggers tipped with beads. Similar toys, such as small riding crops and whips, are also delightful, whether they're part of a costume or actually put to use. Stay gentle: The goal is to please, not bruise.

Night Fourteen
A Touch of the Lash

"I want to ask you something," I said. He smiled lazily, shifting his long legs off of mine. "Why are all the cabinets in here locked?" Within his playroom, silver padlocks hung from every door and drawer.

"My toys are valuable," he said. "I take them out only as needed."

A night of pleasure had put me in an impish mood. "I bet they're empty," I teased, poking him in the ribs. "Mister Mystery. You can't fool me."

He moved to a silver lockbox by the door, input a code on its touchpad, and drew out a laden key ring. How did he keep them all straight? "As I said, I take them out as needed," he said, unlocking a tall cabinet. "And I think they're needed now."

I gazed at the objects he'd retrieved. Strands of silk, rubber, leather ... all black, and bound on silver handles. "Turn over," he said. "Onto your hands and knees." The first touch was gentle, like a breeze. He changed tools and something rougher sweetly stung my buttocks and thighs. "Do you like my toys now, my darling?" The flogger came down again, heating my pale skin like a sunlamp. And I did, oh, yes, I did.

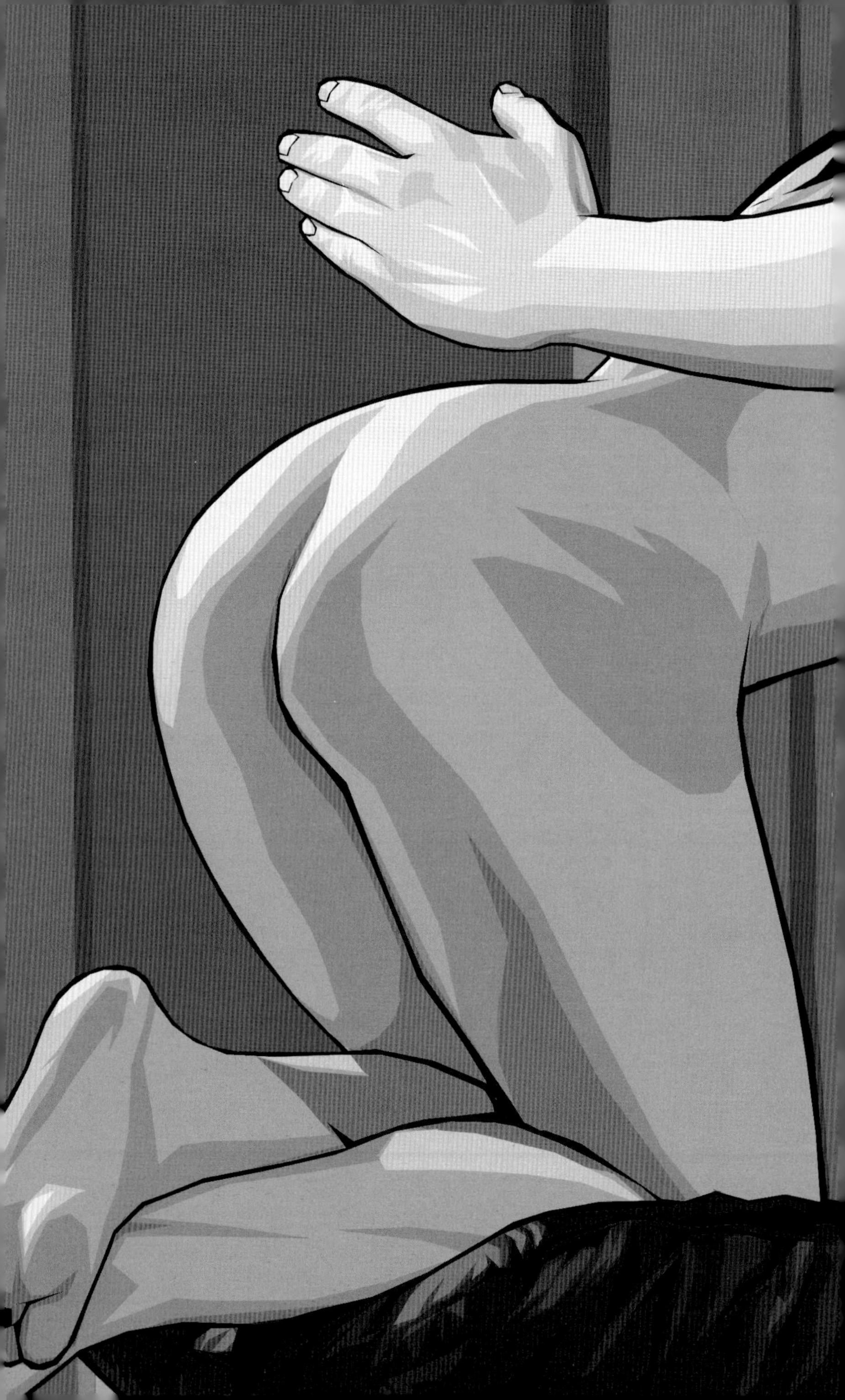

Night Fifteen
Bad Girls Get Spanked

That night, we dined at a classic gentlemen's club high on a city hill. The waiters all knew him by name, and he ordered for me without asking what I wanted.

"You look lovely in that dress," he said, cutting into his steak. I glanced down at what I wore for him. It was mist-colored, short, and tight. As I sipped my wine, I felt his hand slip between my knees. He moved higher, to the junction of my thighs, then halted. "You've disobeyed me," he said menacingly. "You're wearing panties."

"But this dress is practically transparent..."

"I decide what you wear. And what you don't," he answered, leading me from the dining room, through dark-paneled hallways, to an empty sitting room. "Kneel," he said, indicating a leather ottoman. He lifted my hem, caressing my behind through my lacy panties. "Too bad they're so beautiful," he murmured, then swatted me lightly, and tore them away.

He struck me again, caressing, then slapping a third time. His palm was so hot, and I grew wet despite my anger. "Open your legs," he ordered, and slapped me right there, gently, then firmly. "Will you remember my commands?" he inquired. "Yes, sir," I answered.

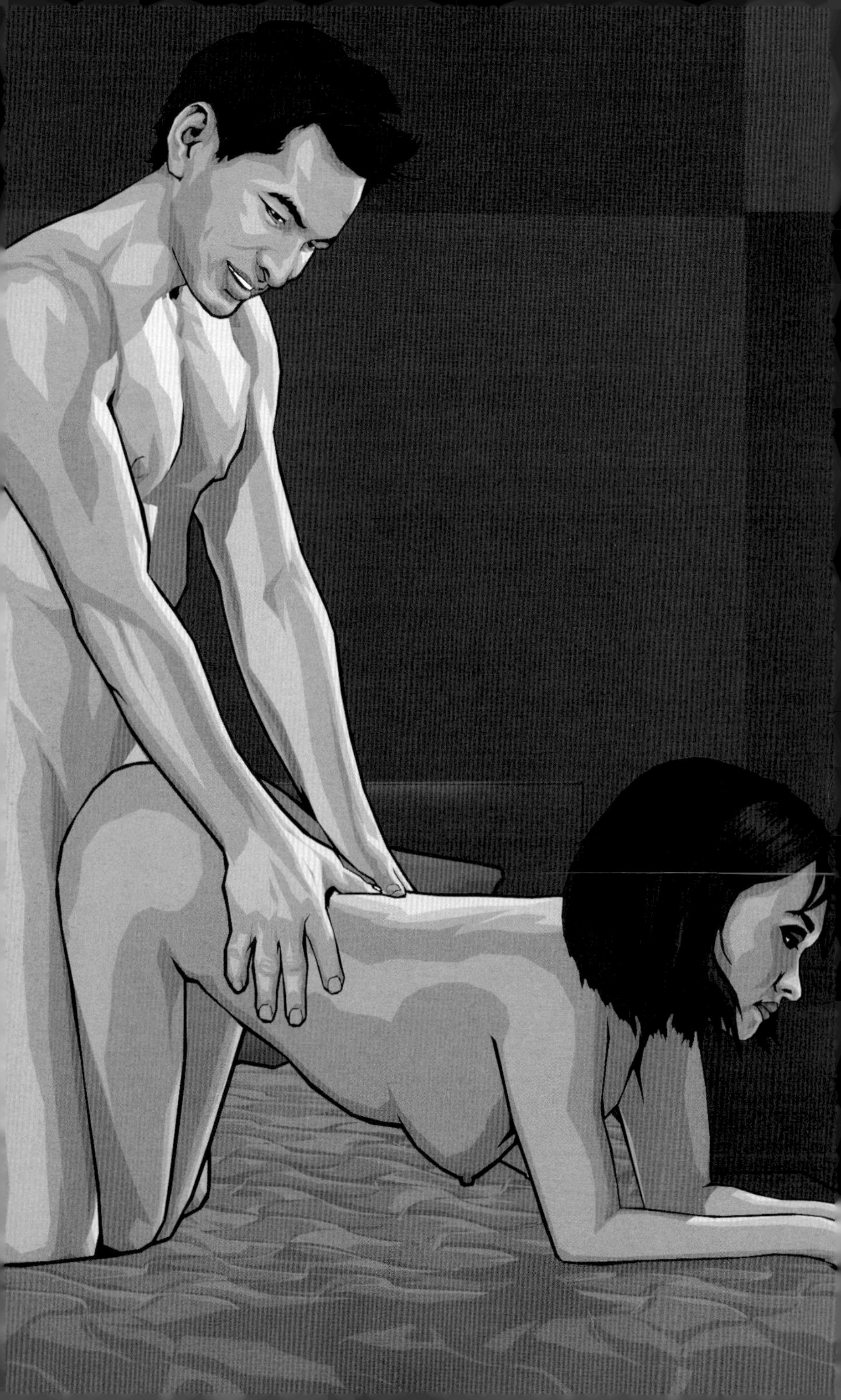

Night Sixteen
Taken from Behind

I stormed into his room, a little crazy with desire. "What's this?" he inquired, turning from his book with one eyebrow raised. "I didn't call for you."

"I don't care," I said, flinging myself face-down on the bed. "Tonight you'll do what I want."

"Will I," he said. It was not a question. I gathered my courage. "Get undressed," I ordered him. He didn't move. "Please, sir," I added. He stood and unzipped his trousers, then raised his black t-shirt, and before I could move, he was behind me, strong hands pulling my hips into the air.

"Giving orders, my love?" he whispered, rubbing his erection in the slippery furrow between my legs. "Maybe you require a firmer lesson tonight." He gripped my legs between his thighs and entered me suddenly.

I melted onto the bed and he shifted back on his heels, wrapping my legs around his hips and slipping into me from an exquisite new angle. I moaned into the dark, raising myself on my arms so he could tease my breasts. As I slowly lost control, he pressed me downward, hand at the back of my neck. "That's right," he murmured, working me ever harder. "That's my good girl."

THE SEXY SECRET:

1. There's no magic trick to fellatio. Playfulness, enthusiasm, and a willingness to experiment are all you need.

2. Start slowly, teasing the head and frenulum—that magic spot where the head meets the underside of the shaft—with the tip of your tongue. Wait until he's really hot before you take all of him in your mouth.

3. Watch his reactions to discern what he wants. Does he like you to grasp his shaft as you suck, or is he a hands-free boy? Does he like a quick, fast motion, or is slow suction his thing?

4. Encourage him to play with you, too. Bring his hands to your breasts or, if you're lying down, straddle him backward in a 69 position so that you can pleasure each other.

Night Seventeen
At Your Service

He began to study my journal each night before he touched me, reading in his armchair while I reclined naked at his feet. "You're progressing well," he said. "But there remain many areas in which more study is needed."

He stood before me and unbuttoned his jeans, drawing out his erection. At eye level he seemed... far too big. "Open your mouth," he commanded. I did, cautiously taking the head of his penis between my lips. He thrust forward and I pulled back a bit, but he cupped my head and pushed again. "Use your tongue, love," he said. "Around the tip, then up and down."

I licked up his shaft and curled my tongue slowly around the head. "That's it, that's it," he breathed. "Now deeper," he said, and I caught his rhythm, opening my mouth widely to take his full length.

He caught my hand in his and raised it to his balls. "These, too," he said, and I palmed them gently, slipping a finger backward to stroke the skin behind. "An excellent pupil," he said between gasps. I wrapped my hands around his hips and drew him closer still, sensing he was under my power now.

THE SEXY SECRET:

1. Deep-throating is a challenge for both partners: The man needs to proceed slowly, and the woman should be willing and relaxed enough to try the trick. (Some women swear by practicing with popsicles or lollipops.)

2. Start by taking his shaft as far into your mouth as possible without gagging. After several minutes—or several sessions—you may be ready to move further.

3. Getting deep-throating right is all about angle. Experiment with different positions and approaches to find the one that works best for your two bodies. The woman can focus on breathing deeply and regularly to relax her throat.

4. Wrapping a hand around the base of the penis allows him to experience this sensation of being fully engulfed without triggering the gag reflex.

Night Eighteen
Deep Love

The night after our lesson in oral pleasure, he led me to his bedroom, where I expected our lessons would take yet another new turn.

Instead, he laid me down at the edge of the bed, face up, and caressed my throat with his hands and lips until I inclined my head slightly backward. "Stage two of last night's lesson, my sweet," he breathed. He was rising again, his erection growing before my eyes.

"Relax your neck," he instructed, guiding himself between my lips. He moved slowly, a bit deeper each time. "I want to see how much you can take."

He bent over me, moving farther still into the back of my mouth. The sensation was strange but thrilling as he pushed eagerly inward. I could sense that he longed to thrust harder, yet he reined himself in. I tipped my head back, willing myself to relax my throat, wanting all of him. He slipped deeper, unbelievably deeper. I reached over my head to clasp his strong thighs, pulling until the sweet, musky base of his shaft was against my lips and he emptied into my throat, growling like a lion.

NIGHT NINETEEN
Helpless with Pleasure

I was fuming by the time I heard his keys in the door. It was midnight. "Where have you been?" I shouted down the hallway, aware of the jealousy in my voice. Had he been with someone else?

He sauntered in and set down his briefcase. "Business," he said. "My business, and not yours." He loosened his tie and undressed slowly; my rage soon drowned under a rising tide of lust. He lay across the bed and sighed, draping a forearm over his eyes. He was exhausted, I realized.

Abashed, I stroked his strong abdomen and legs, caressing him with my palm. His penis stirred—at least one part of him wasn't tired. I drew it toward my mouth. "I'll send you to sleep with a smile, my love," I said softly. Then, without warning, he drew away. "What's the matter?" I asked. "Did I do something wrong?"

"Not at all, my darling. Turn around and straddle me." I did as he commanded, and he drew my hips toward his face. Oh, my. I felt his tongue stroking me, circling my clitoris, as I returned my mouth to his swollen erection. Soon, his skill overtook mine and I came, in great shuddering bursts.

My orgasm finished, I moved to roll away, to continue sucking him from a new angle. "Where do you think you're going?" he said, grabbing my hips and forcing me back onto him. "I ... I'm done," I stammered.

"You're done when I say you're done," he growled, sinking his fingers into my flesh. "I am going to get at least another orgasm out of you. Maybe two. Or three. How do you like that?"

I protested that I wasn't sure my body could comply, but his only response was to redouble his efforts. Gradually I found my pace in our dance, caressing him with my mouth while his tongue and fingers swept my clitoris, finding their way inside me. Hot energy circled around and through us, building in perfect harmony toward the inevitable explosion ... over and over again.

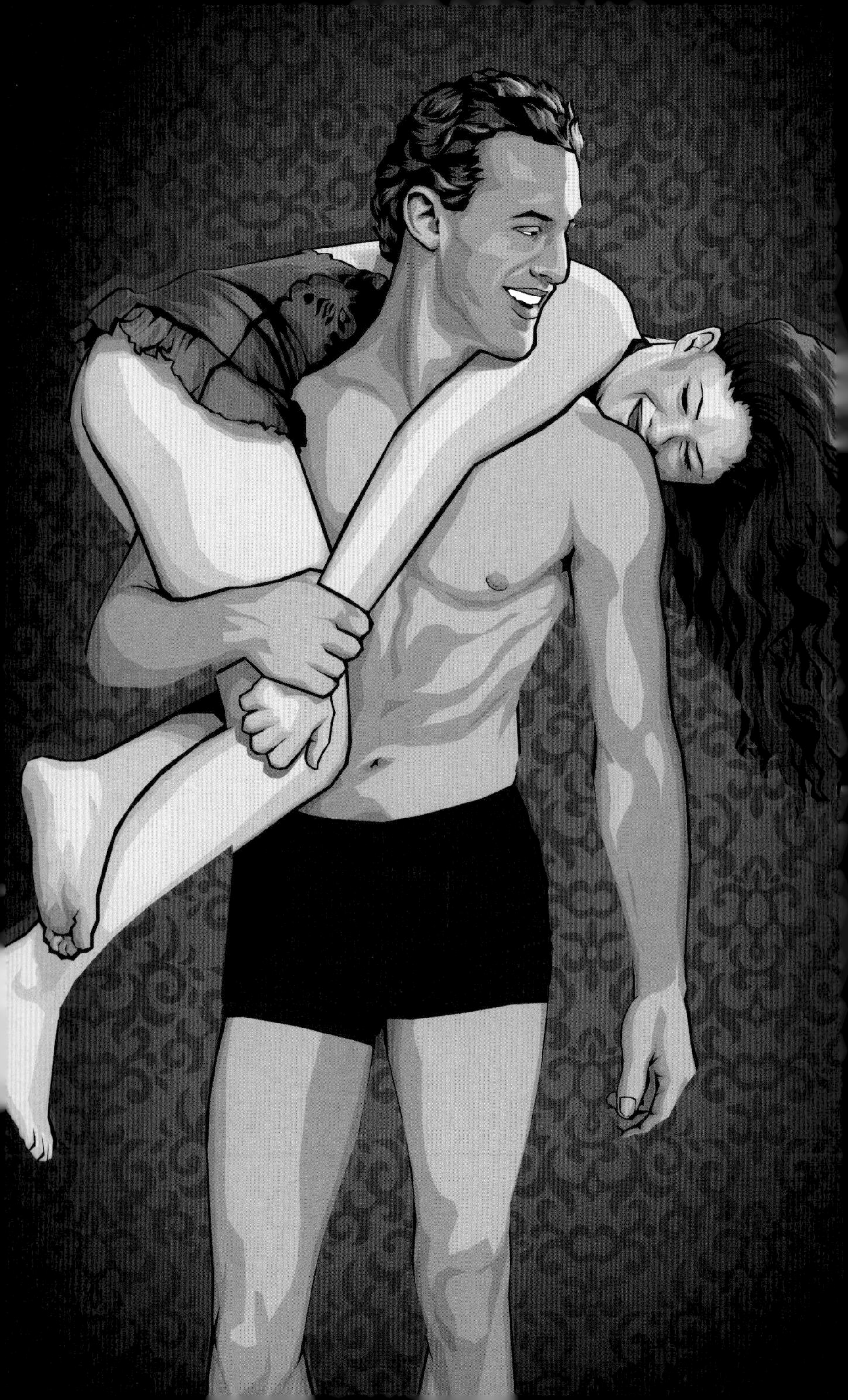

NIGHT TWENTY
Swept Off My Feet

He stepped back, eyeing me from head to foot. I glimpsed myself in the playroom's wide mirror, feeling foolish. The scrap of fuchsia taffeta he'd dressed me in was split to the crotch, saved from obscenity only by a flimsy black g-string below it.

"I look like a lap dancer," I groaned.

"You look... unbelievable," he said, drawing a fingertip down the deep V of the neckline. Somehow even this made me cranky. "No," I said, starting to pull the thing off me and move away. "I don't want this tonight." Even as I said it, I knew it wasn't true. And he sensed it too. He knew me far too well.

Before I reached the door, he'd knelt down and grasped my arm, flinging me bodily across his shoulders. I gasped. He was even stronger than I'd realized. He easily stood, my weight across him, clasping me in place with a single firm hand. He turned to smile at me. "Where to, my love?" he whispered. "Shall I carry you home?"

"No," I said, smiling against his shoulder, loving the sensation of weightlessness. "Carry me... to bed."

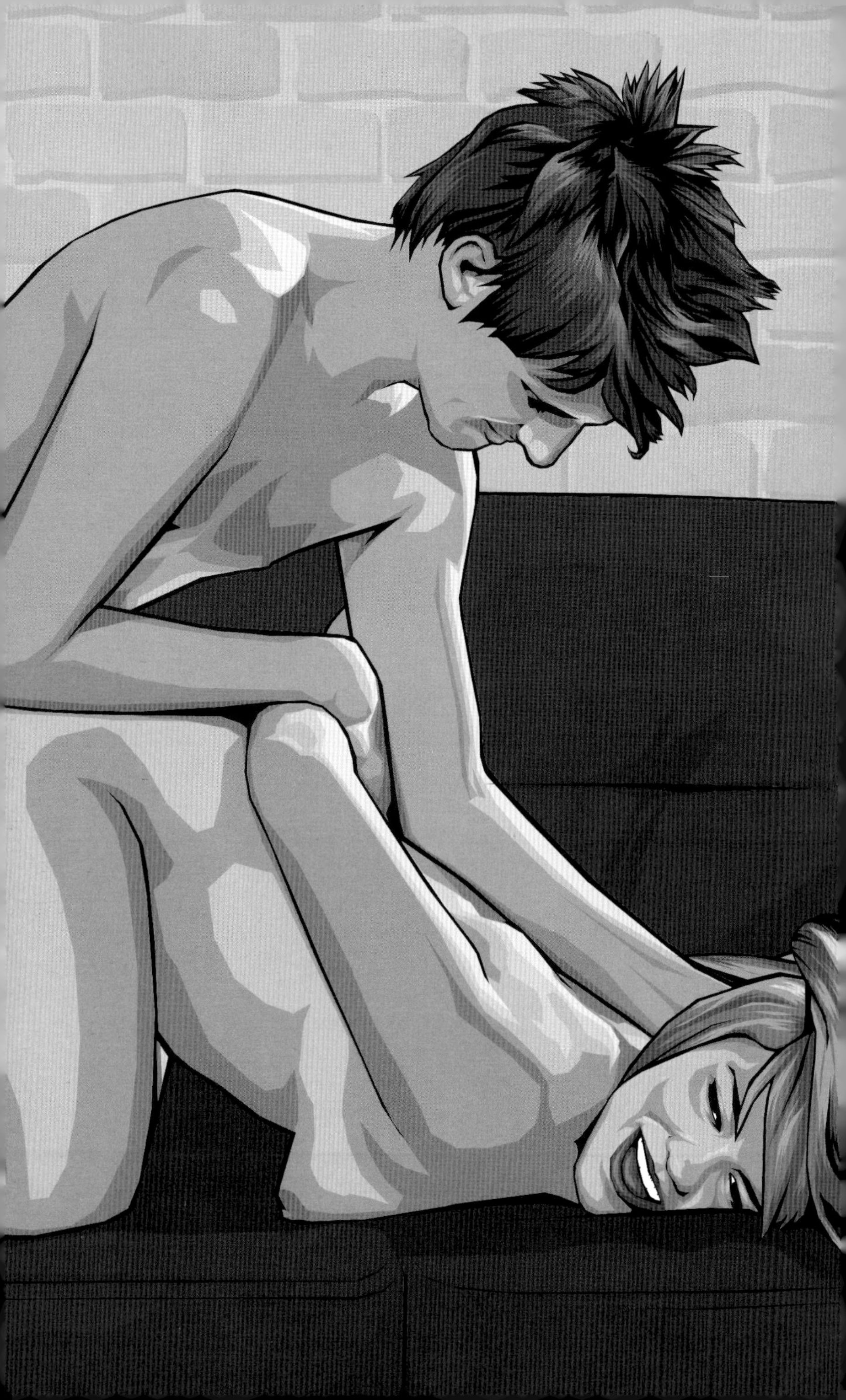

Night Twenty-One
A Firm Hand

The city was humid, and I was weary of my long, heavy hair. I made a few sketches, penciling in my features topped with a series of pixie cuts and bobs.

Once he glimpsed them, he frowned. "Considering a cut?" he asked. I drew my hair forward over my face, eyeing him saucily through its strands.

He turned me around and took my hairbrush from my purse. Slowly, he brushed my hair, smoothing it into a long, glossy ponytail. "Thank you," I sighed, leaning against him. Then a hard swat on my bottom from the flat side of the hairbrush brought me upright again.

He stripped off my dress and pushed me down onto the couch, my bottom high in the air. "Keep your hair long," he breathed into my neck. He pinned my arm behind my back, and gathered up the ponytail, tugging it like reins. My heart raced as he nipped me lightly on the shoulders and nape of the neck. "I require a harness when I ride," he said, twisting my hair harder in his fist.

I laughed into the cushions, amused and aroused. "Yes, sir," I assented. "If it means so much to him, a harness my master shall have."

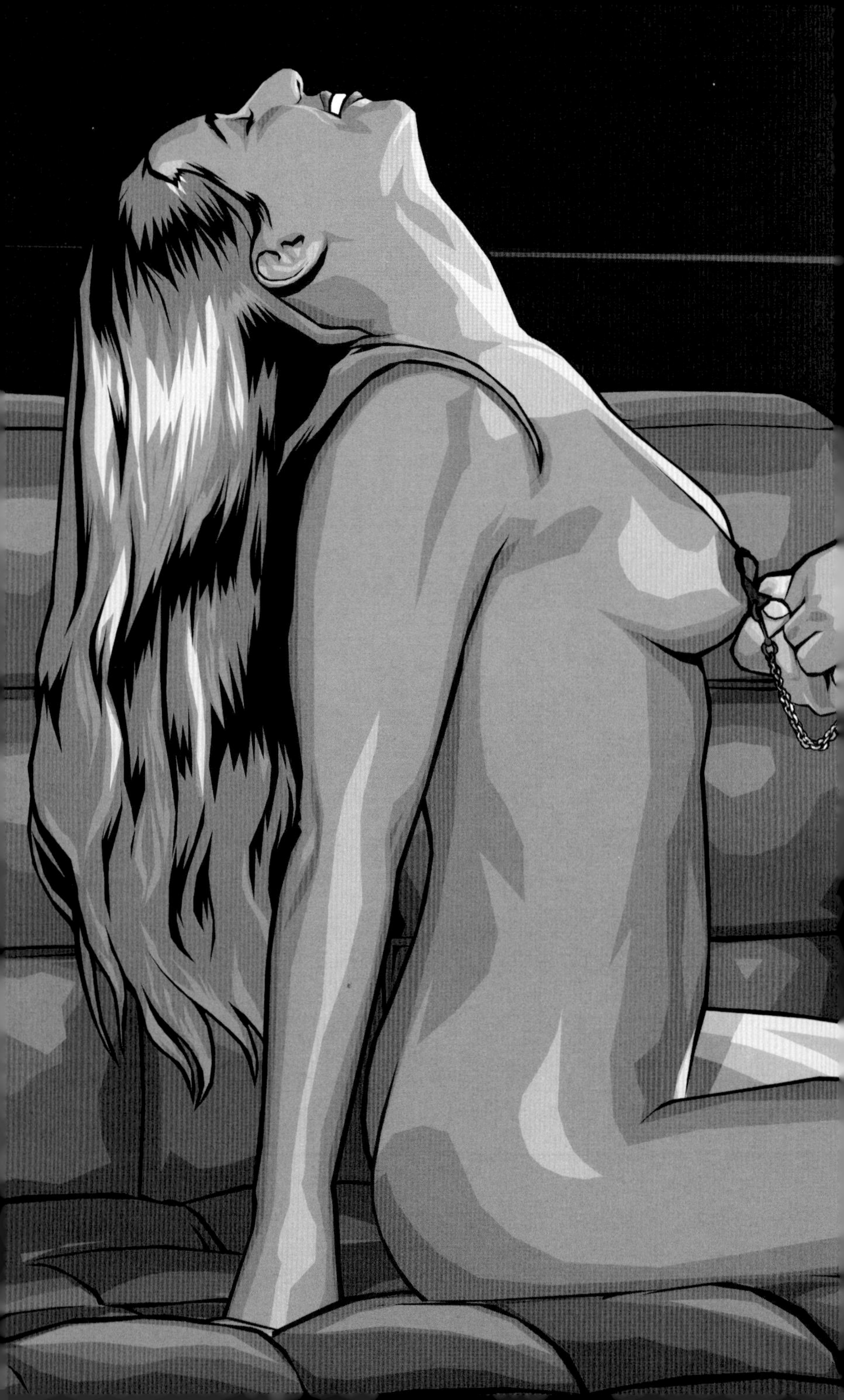

Night Twenty-Two
Pain Becomes Pleasure

"Lean back. No, farther. Arch your back. Let me see those beautiful nipples." I knelt, anticipating his touch, my nipples already erect at the thought of what might come next, remembering his pinching and teasing that had seemed so cruel at first. "Close your eyes," he ordered.

He cupped my breast in his hand, and I felt a pinch—a pinch that grew steadily firmer, teetering on the edge between exciting and painful. "This is a tweezer clip," he told me. "For beginners. I'm going easy on you, for now."

He attached a metal clip to each nipple, a chain dangling between them. As I arched my back, presenting myself to him, he gently tugged the chain, causing me to gasp in surprise. "So, you like this?" he asked. I whimpered my cautious assent, afraid of what too enthusiastic a response might mean to him.

"Well, then," he laughed. "Let's try something a little more intense." I heard the jingling of chains as he brought out the next set of clamps...

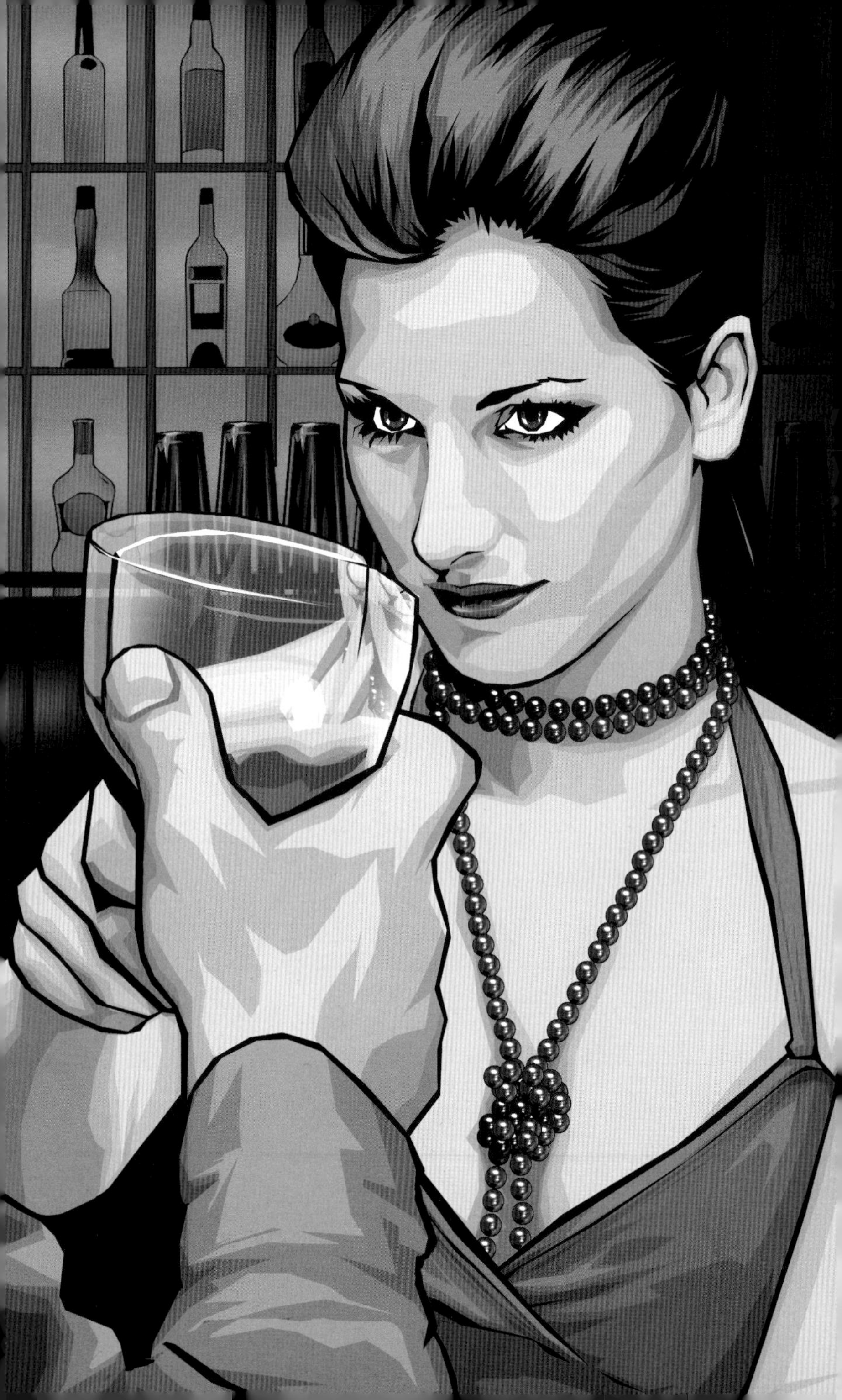

NIGHT TWENTY-THREE
You Will Meet a Stranger

He'd asked me to meet him at a plush downtown lounge. Clad in the scarlet dress that I knew he liked best, the one that teased the line between elegant and provocative, I swirled my wine slowly, waiting. Tonight I had a plan for him.

Soon, he strode through the door—I assessed him as I would a stranger. Tall. Broad shoulders. A confident air to his walk. Yes, a promising candidate. He took the seat next to me as if he owned it, and leaned in for a kiss. I drew back. "Have we met?" I inquired politely.

He sat back, amusement flickering in his dark eyes. "I don't believe we have, miss," he replied. "I must have mistaken you for someone else." The bartender placed a whiskey before him and he raised it in a toast, his glance running over my body. "Allow me to introduce myself," he said. "I'm a traveling businessman."

"And what business might you be in?" I asked.

"I provide certain services," he said, shifting so his thigh brushed mine. "You might say I assist in filling open positions."

"Well, then," I said, beckoning the waiter to refill his glass, "I have a vacancy that might interest you."

THE SEXY SECRET:

1. Threesomes are hot but combustible fun. So that no one gets hurt, talk beforehand to ensure that everyone is truly willing to play. Agree with your partner what you will and won't do. Maybe intercourse with the other woman is off the table; maybe the man isn't allowed to kiss the newcomer. Set parameters: Will this be a one-off booty call or a three-way love affair in the making?

2. Dole out attention according to whatever arrangement feels best. Anyone who's giving pleasure—fellatio, cunnilingus—should be getting it, too, via intercourse or hand work.

3. Work for a relaxed three-way rhythm rather than trying every contortion in the book. After all, if everyone's comfortable, happy, and gets off, you can set up future playdates for still-wilder scenes.

NIGHT TWENTY-FOUR
The Rule of Three

"That one?" he asked, amused. "No, that one," I insisted, pointing to a slender, raven-haired woman moving lithely across the dance floor. It had taken him days to coax me into this particular lesson, and now I was determined to choose for both of us.

"Madame's orders," he said and slipped into the crowd. I watched them dance together, his fingers first brushing her long neck, then her back, then lowering to cup her small buttocks. She's his, I thought, with a rising wave of jealousy and desire. He could ask her to do anything and she would, right there and then. He whispered in her ear, pointed at me, and she cast me a teasing smile.

That smile returned a few hours later, as she ducked her head between my thighs to caress me with her tongue. I moaned, parting my legs farther. It was so different with a woman—everything was so soft. I glimpsed him in the shadows behind her. He caressed her rear, then entered her from behind, gazing down at her lips working me into a frenzy. "I think she's ready for you now," she said. She rose over me, pulling my hands to her silky mound, and he slipped from her body straight into mine.

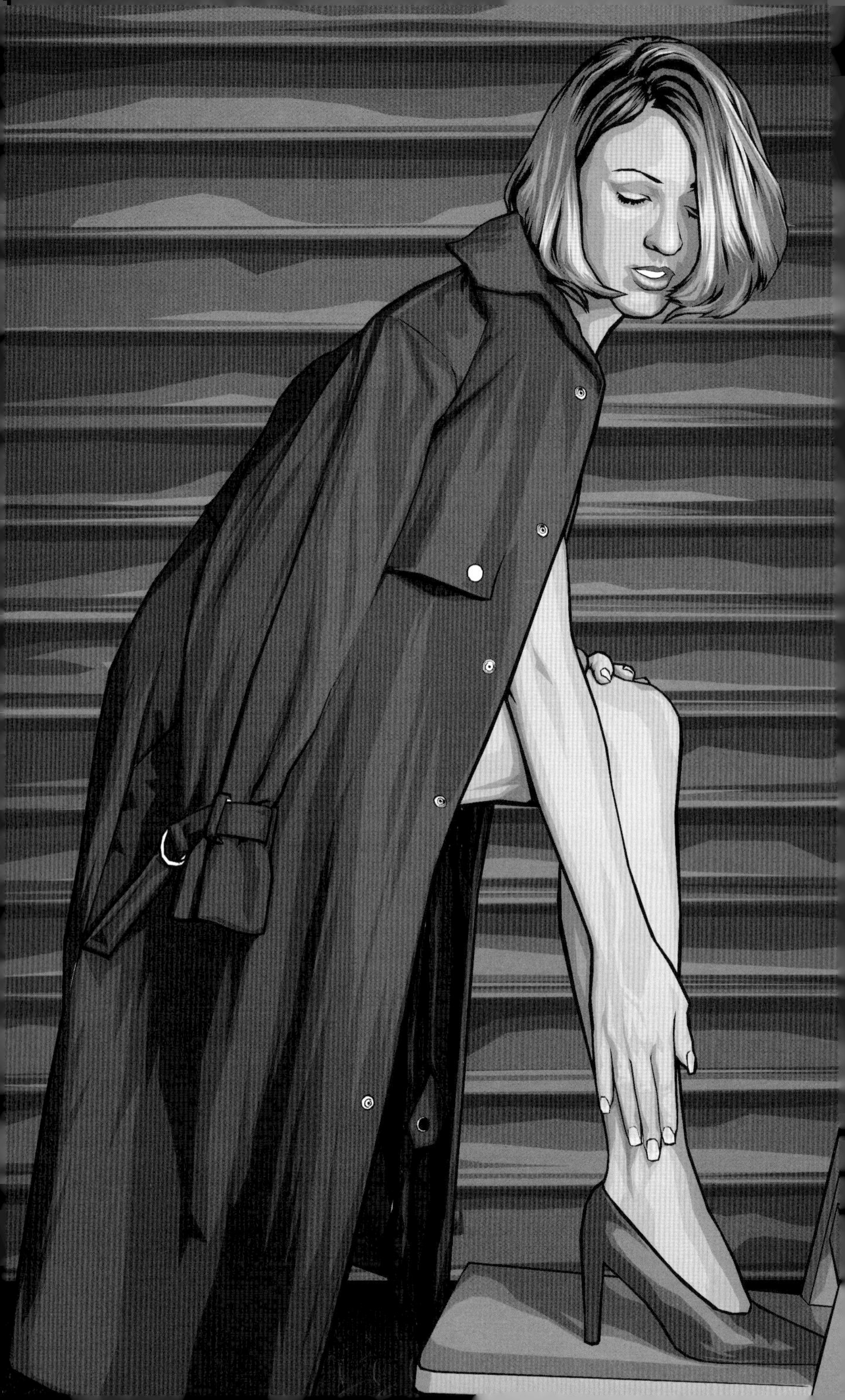

NIGHT TWENTY-FIVE
The Girl in the Long Red Coat

Our relationship was at a new milestone: He'd invited me to dinner with his colleagues. We arrived at a stark modern loft, all marble and steel, and his coworkers and their elegant wives greeted me curiously, assessingly. Our host offered to help me out of my long silk coat, but I declined. "I get so chilly in big houses," I apologized, smiling politely.

As we filed into dinner, he jerked me around a corner, into a dark hallway. "What are you playing at?" he hissed. I opened my lapels, pressing my naked breasts forward. "This," I whispered seductively.

"Now, of all times?" he snapped. "Do you understand where we are, who we're with?"

"I understand perfectly," I said, unbelting the coat. Underneath, I was bare and smooth, right down to my blood-red pumps. He gasped with frustration and yanked the coat shut, buttoning it tightly before we entered the dining room. I smiled through the first course, knowing he'd be stroking my thigh before the entrée, fingering me during dessert, and taking me—hard—in that dark hallway while his colleagues sipped cognac and wondered who, exactly, I was.

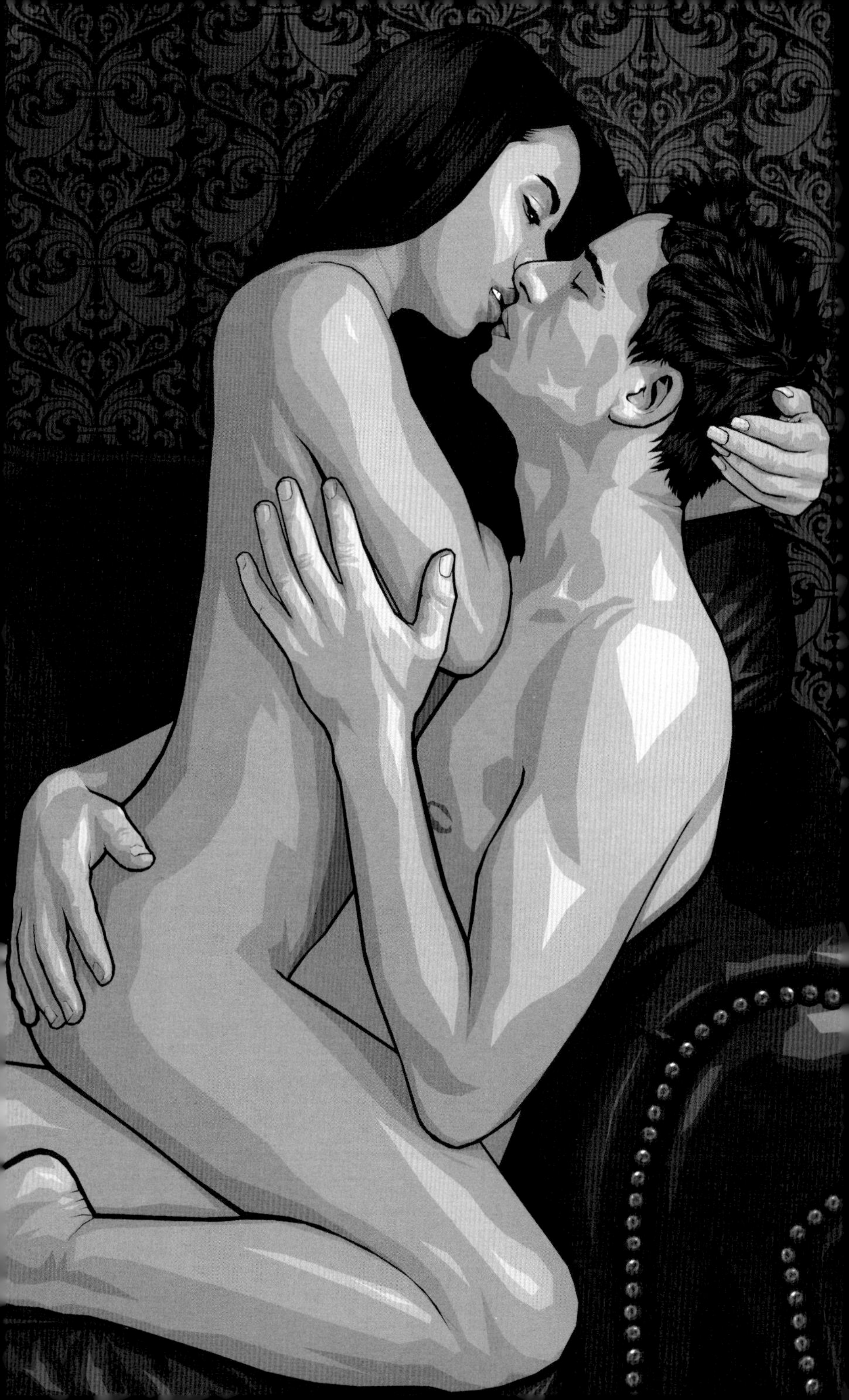

NIGHT TWENTY-SIX
The Changing of the Guard

My journal was filled with photographs, drawings, stories of what he done with me, and details of my dreams and fantasies filled its pages to overflowing. We entwined on the couch, exhausted after hours of riding each other, and he read aloud from it, praising my conscientious work.

I rolled on top of him. "I've graduated, then," I said. "My studies are complete."

"One's studies are never complete," he replied. "I plan to teach you for the rest of your life." He shifted under me, ready to begin again, but I halted him.

"Tomorrow I'll be sending a blank notebook to you, instead," I announced. "And I expect you to fill it just as I did. It's my turn to play teacher, darling, and yours to play the dutiful student." He considered the idea, laughter lurking somewhere in his dark eyes.

"And one more thing," I said, running a finger down his sweating chest. "I'll need the keys."

"Which keys?"

"The keys to your playroom, darling. I'm going to turn it into my classroom, with you as my student."

THE SEXY SECRET:

1. Sample a nibble or a light bite of your lover during foreplay to see if he enjoys a taste of pain with his pleasure. If he does, bite slightly harder and ask if he'd like more.

2. Shoulders, the nape of the neck, the tender insides of arms and thighs, toes and fingers: Everything's fair game for a gentle bite. Work them in unexpectedly to jolt your lover—try nipping him during his orgasm, when even painful sensations can feel pleasurable.

Night Twenty-Seven
A Foretaste of Pleasure

On the floor in the playroom, I nibbled lightly at his bare toes, still damp from our languorous bath together. He squirmed, ticklish, so I increased the pressure, nipping him hard on the instep, then running my long fingernails up the back of his calf, along his thigh, and to his well-muscled abdomen. I lingered there a moment, watching his erection, knowing what he anticipated.

Yet I bypassed that temptation and moved onward, sweeping my lips across his, biting him lightly along his jawline and then on one ear. That pleased him—he shifted in his chair, reaching for my hands. I moved out of range and stood behind him. Then I leaned over, grasped his erection in one hand, and softly placed my teeth on his neck. "Would I make a good vampire?" I breathed.

"No," he said, moving against my hand. "You'd be wonderfully evil." I bit him harder, sensing the blood pulsing just beneath his skin.

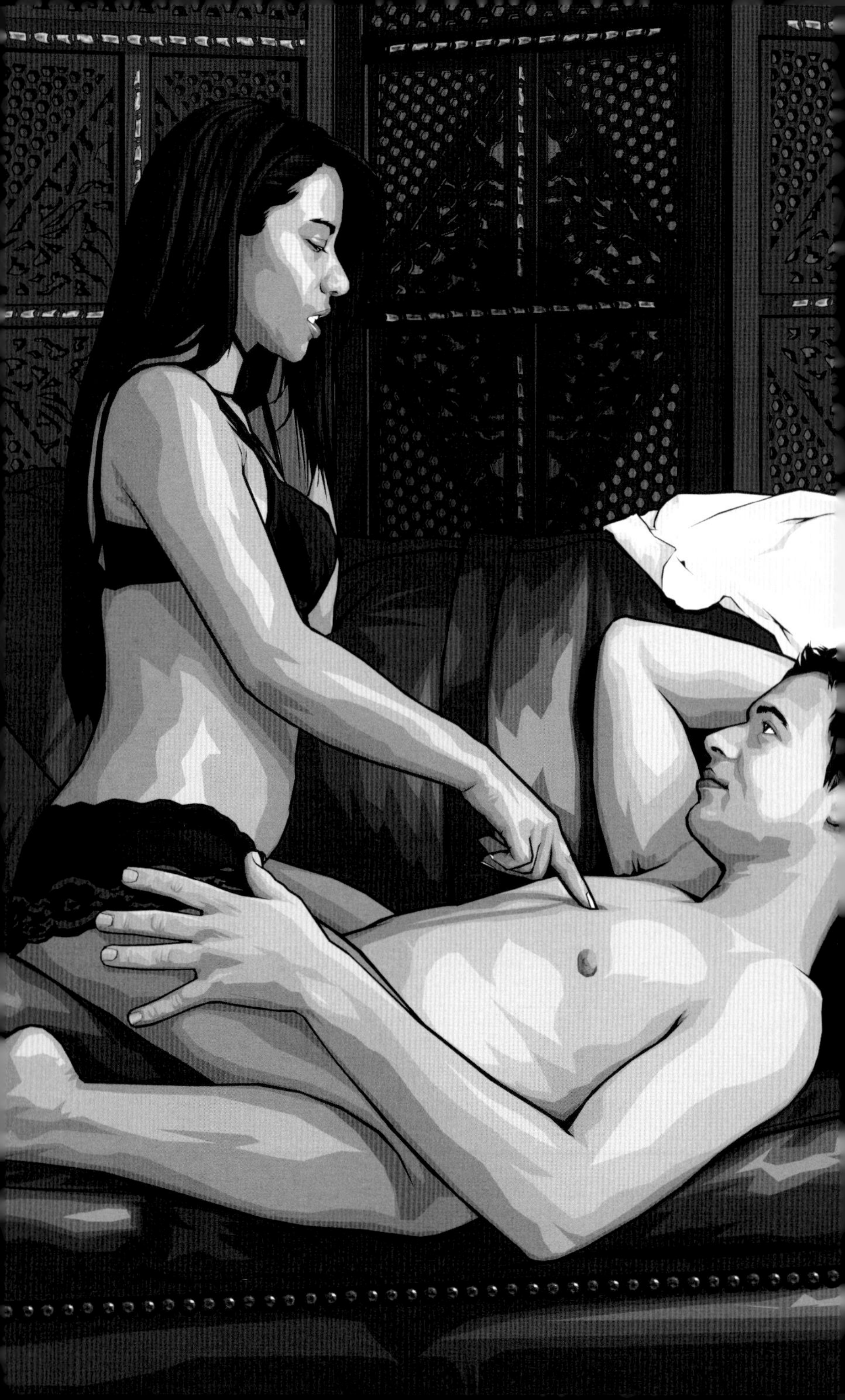

Night Twenty-Eight
Story Hour

I stripped for him on the balcony that evening, letting the wind take each bit of clothing. Away went the silk stockings he'd bought me. My silver dress swirled into the night, off to shock whoever would find it the next morning.

As I entered the apartment, he reached for me, but I pushed him to the couch. "I won't let you touch me tonight," I said, straddling him. He groaned in frustration. "Instead I'll tell you a bedtime story for your journal.

"Once, there was a proud prince who ruled from a grand castle. One day, while he was out riding, a golden-haired witch called to him from the woods. Drawn by her beauty, he went to her, but she cast a spell upon him and he fell into sleep.

"He awoke in a cell, chained to an iron bed by his wrists and ankles. There he remained for days." I worked my hand between his legs. "Every evening, the beautiful witch entered the dungeon to feed him honey and bread"—I kissed him lightly down his chest and stomach—"and use her enchantments to take his power for her potions. After all, nothing is stronger than the seed of a prince." And I closed my lips around him.

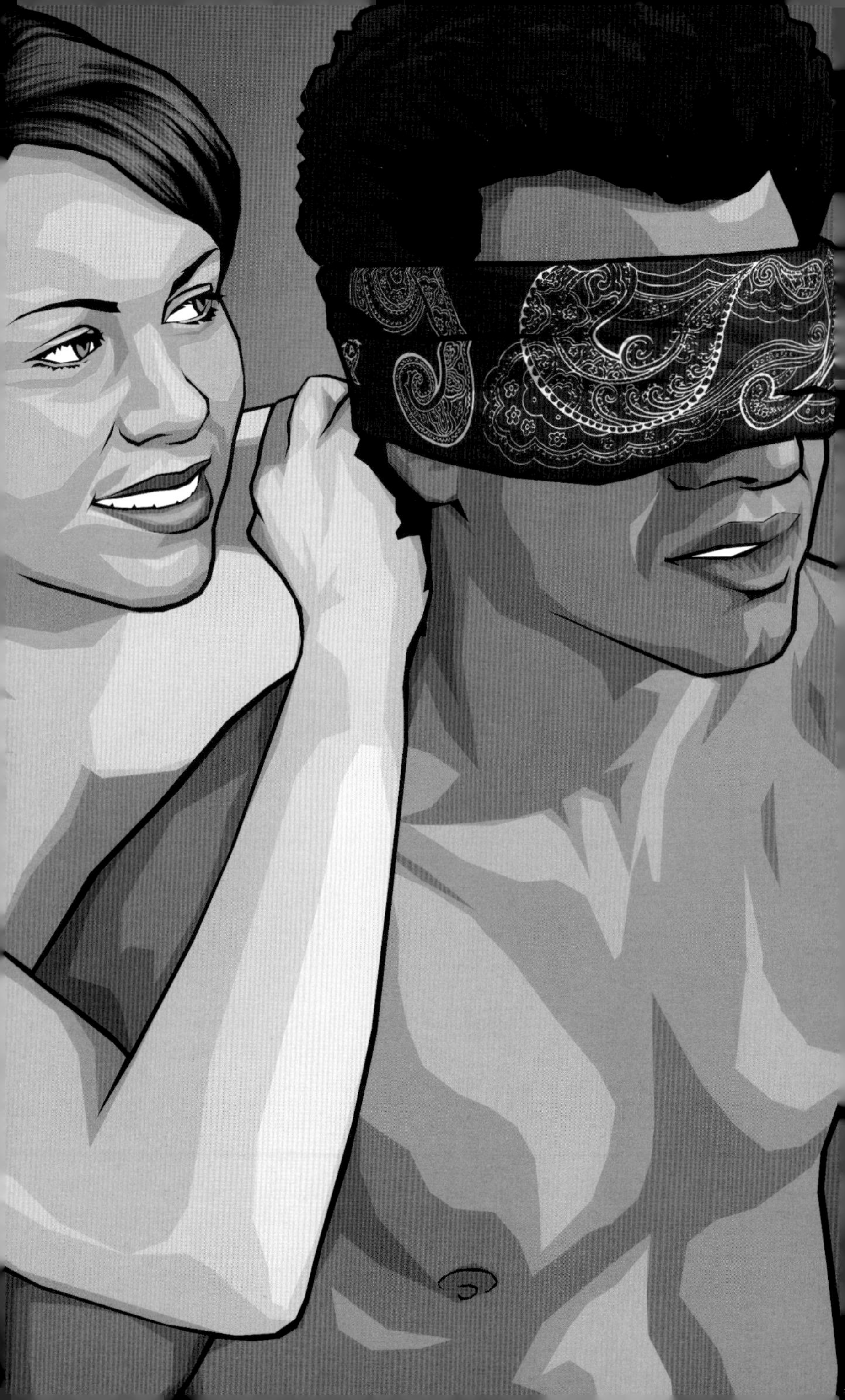

Night Twenty-Nine
Trust Me

At dinner he found beside his cutlery not a napkin, but a heavy silk scarf. He turned it over in his hands, amused. "This is a serious lesson," I told him. "No smirking." I folded the scarf and bound it tightly over his eyes.

"Am I to eat this way, madame?" he inquired.

"You are," I replied. From the kitchen, I brought out a platter prepared earlier that day and set it before him. I enjoyed his hesitation as he speared at the morsels before him—he didn't know precisely what he was putting into his mouth, and I knew it made him nervous. Afterward, I ordered him to walk to the playroom. He moved cautiously, hands outstretched, and in the room he undressed with awkward hands.

"Now you may pleasure me," I announced, reclining on the bed. He knelt and reached for me, stroking my legs. "You feel ... unfamiliar." He caressed me with strangely cautious fingers. "You could be anyone."

"Very true. I could be anyone at all. A stranger." I offered my breast to one of his searching hands and moved his other hand between my legs. "Maybe someone you can trust. Or maybe I'm someone ... dangerous."

THE SEXY SECRET:

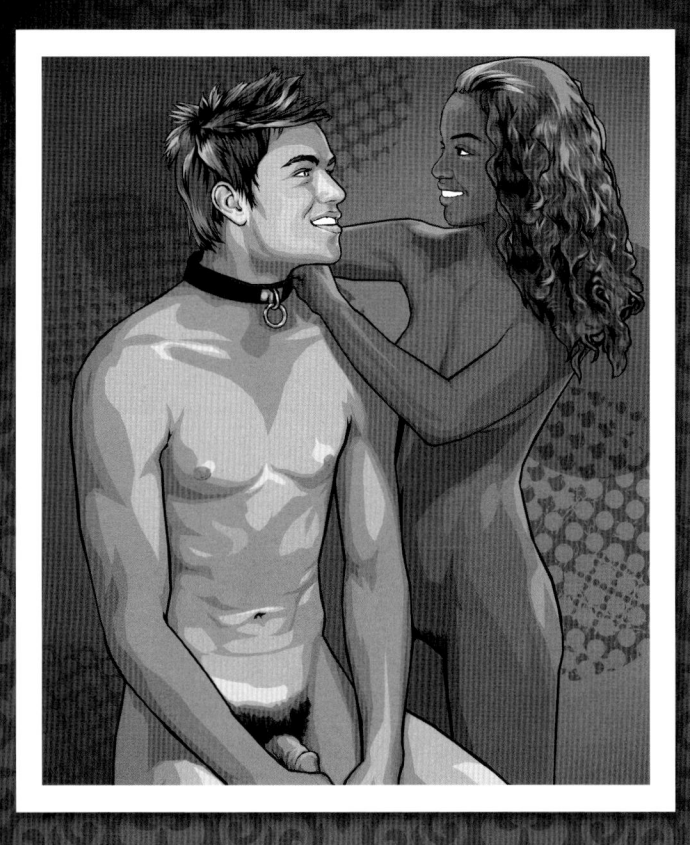

1. Has he been a good boy? Reward him with his own collar of leather, rubber, or stainless steel. Most include hooks, rings, and locks so you can add accessories such as leashes and chains that link to other restraint devices. Look for those that are easily adjustable via buckles or D-rings and fit your partner loosely.

2. Collar your man for a single night of play, or, if he's seriously into being "owned," ask him to wear it in public. Consider adding a symbol of your relationship, such as a medallion bearing your name, or an image that has meaning to both of you. You can also buy him a necklace that looks conventional but has secret significance to the two of you.

Night Thirty
Taking the Collar

I arched above him, sliding slowly up and down his erection. He tried to hold me in place, to make me work faster, and I peeled his hands off my hips and set them gently on the sheet. "Against the rules," I reminded him.

I slid off him, using his shaft to stroke myself toward my own orgasm while delaying his. The heat grew and circled inside me, I pressed my mouth to his, and I came, whispering his name. "Damn it," he gasped, and tried to roll me over and take me again.

I stopped him. "Are you mine?" I asked.

"Anything you say," he replied. "Just finish." Instead I rose and opened a cabinet by the bed, rummaging through his finely crafted exotic toys.

I found what I needed and returned to the bed. I asked again, "Are you mine?" He nodded assent, and I clasped the thick black leather collar around his neck. To its heavy front ring, I clipped a length of metal chain—a leash. I wrapped it in my fist and slid down upon him again, taking him into me fully and suddenly. "Mine," I breathed, gently tugging the chain as he raised his hips and found release.

THE SEXY SECRET:

1. Starter bondage kits are an ideal way to learn to tie him up. The cuffs attach to bed frames and other furniture, and some include straps so you can tie cuffs together (binding ankles to wrists, for example). Ensure he's comfortable and that he knows you'll free him if he tires of the game.

2. Once your partner's in position, strip before him, touch yourself until you're both aroused, and detail what you'll do to him.

3. Stroke him lightly with your hands, a flogger, or a scarf. Tease him thoroughly before you give him what he's longing for.

4. Explore the exotic reaches of bondage—from spreader bars and x-frames that hold limbs in place to suspension or the intricate art of kinbaku (complex, aesthetic Japanese rope play). Advanced bondage is not to be undertaken lightly, but classes and online resources abound.

Night Thirty-One
In My Hands

I slowly wore away his defenses that night, allowing him to take me as he used to do. I knelt across pillows with my face pressed into the bed as he thrust into me from behind. After his orgasm, I slid quickly downward took him into my mouth until he was hard again, working him slowly until he came a second time.

After he fell deeply asleep, I collected what I required from the intricate cabinets. I slipped one leather cuff around his wrist and fastened it to the headboard, then did the same with his other wrist before his eyes flickered open. He knew immediately what I'd done; he'd done it to me many nights himself. I knelt at the end of the bed, clasping his ankles and spreading his legs. "Do you want this?" I inquired. He was silent. "I won't continue until you say, 'I want this. Bind me.'"

He was quiet. "I want this," he finally said.

"And the rest."

"Bind me." I did. One cuff to each ankle. He was spread-eagled, skin pale against the scarlet bedspread. I snapped on the light over the bed so I could see him clearly, and I told him, precisely, obscenely, what I would do to him in the hours before dawn.

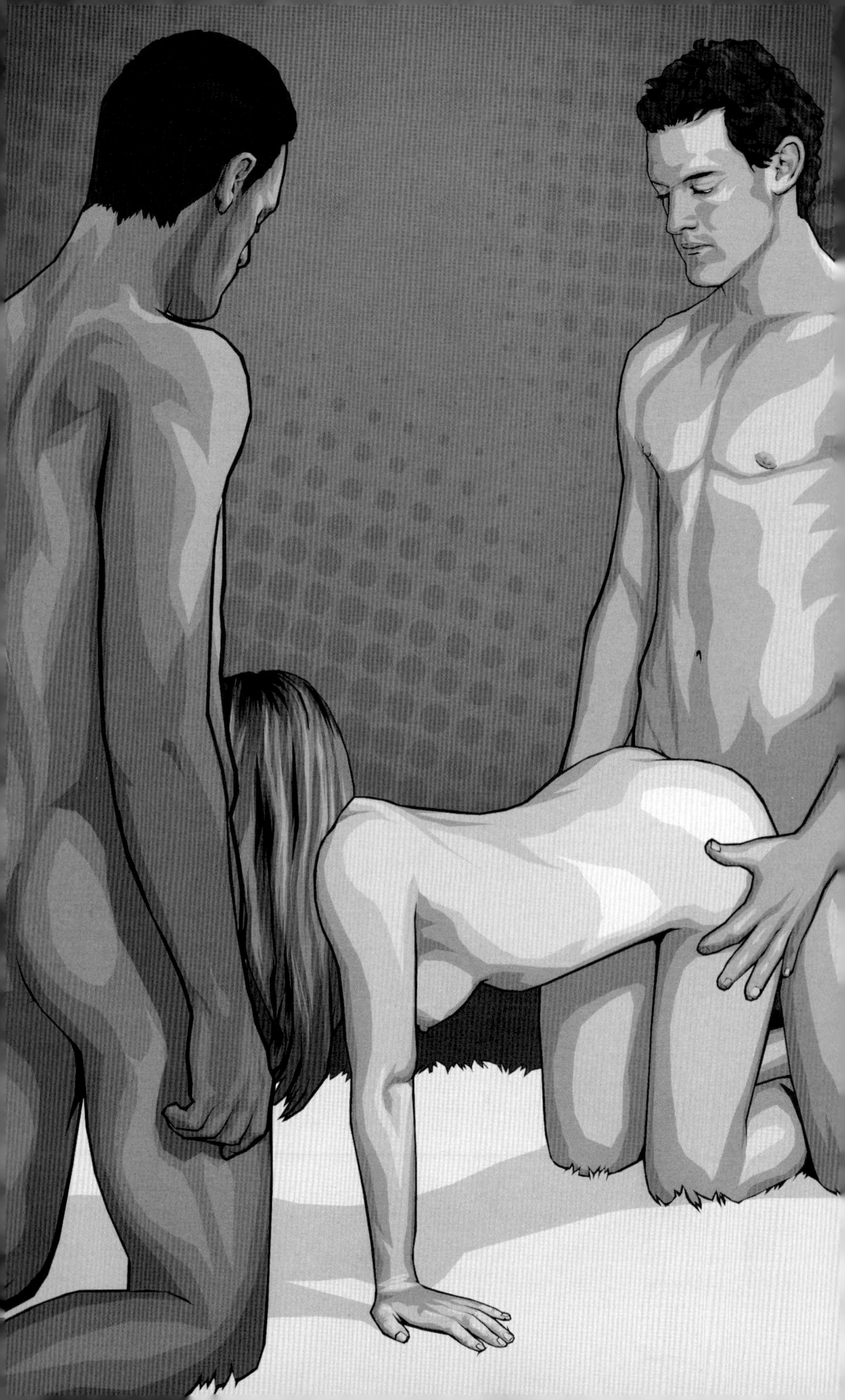

Night Thirty-Two
Caught in the Middle

"Another man, with us?" He blanched when I broached the idea. "I don't want to share you."

"Josh is an old friend. Zero competition. And you've never been with a man. That's a blank page in your lesson book." I took his chin in my hand and kissed him hard. "I don't allow blank pages."

In the playroom that night, my stubborn lover sulked in his chair until he saw me take Josh's eager erection into my mouth. He leaned forward to watch, and Josh tilted his hips to give him a clear view of my lips and tongue caressing his shaft. Lust and tension rose together in his face, and Josh held his gaze, challenging him.

At last my lover stood up and grabbed my hips, spanking me hard and then entering me. I continued to pleasure Josh, and I could sense the war of glares between the two men above me, each moving faster and harder. Who would come first was the unanswered question in the air. Meanwhile I arched my back in delight, loving the struggle between them that played out in my body, and realized that, in fact, I would be the first to go over that edge.

THE SEXY SECRET:

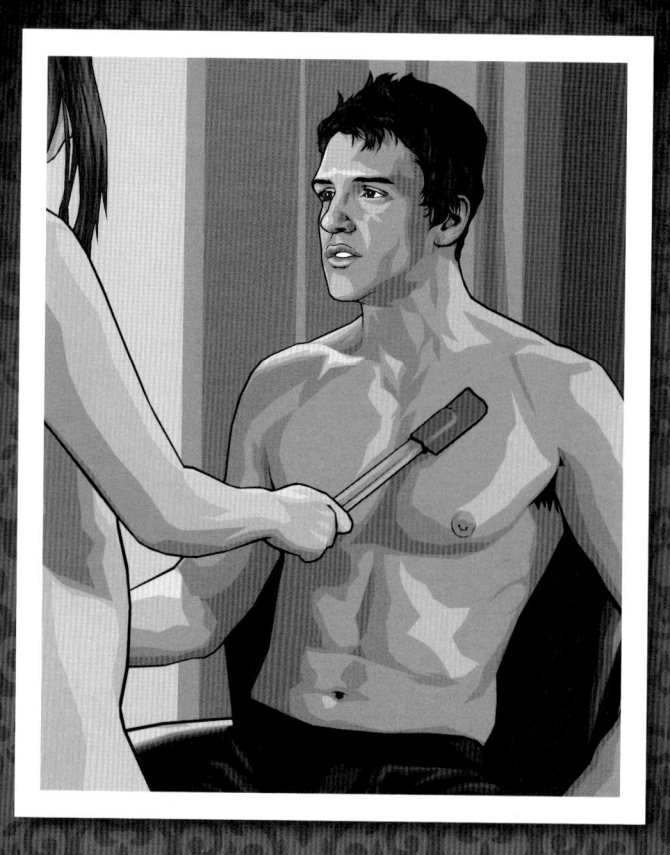

1. If your partner desires a good paddling, you can indulge him with household swatters—anything from a Ping-Pong paddle to the Oxford English Dictionary will bring roses to his cheeks. Or choose from among the plethora of leather, rubber, and wood paddles available at sex shops.

2. As in all pain play, easy does it at first. He might like the sensation—and slight humiliation—or find it too painful. Begin with a few swats peppered with caresses. If your play grows more intense, reserve strong paddling only for buttocks and thighs. Elsewhere, soft pats are the rule.

3. After you've gotten him nice and red, soothe away his hurt with thorough, gentle kisses.

Night Thirty-Three
Taking Your Licks

That night he wrote industriously in his journal, while I idled, sipping wine at the kitchen counter, considering how to use him next. I was delighted and surprised by his willingness to be dominated, as if I'd tapped a wellspring inside him that neither of us had known existed.

When he finished writing, I curled my fingers in his hair as I read aloud: "Tonight, madame, I wish to begin a new tradition. Each evening, at a time you choose, you will order me to fetch you a paddle. Use it on me as you see fit, and if I do not thank you thoroughly afterward, please continue until I do." I laughed. "You've really been dreaming of this?" He nodded, slightly flushed. "Let's make it more interesting," I said. "When you make this request I'll improvise with whatever's at hand."

He smiled as if he'd been hoping for that answer, then reached behind me to a kitchen drawer. He drew out a simple kitchen spatula, unbuttoned his shirt and put the handle in my hand. "Please," he asked. I lifted the thing experimentally, then brought it down on his skin. The sound was abrupt and pleasing. Together we wondered at the scarlet mark on his chest, and where it might lead us.

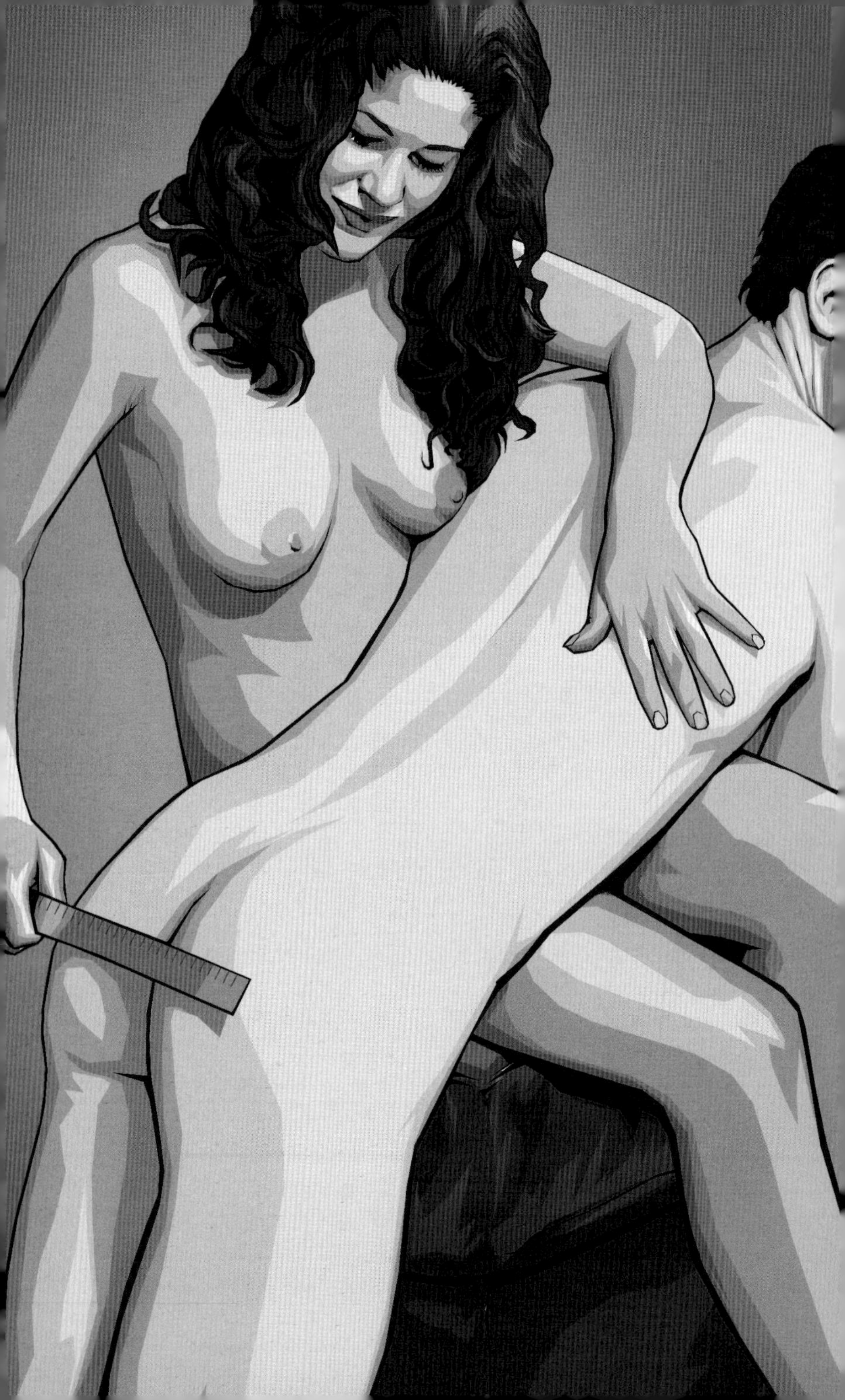

Night Thirty-Four
Teacher Needs to See You After School

In the playroom I presided in a severe gray wool suit, hair bundled high, tiny spectacles perched on my nose. He knelt before me, head down, hands on his knees. "You failed the final," I informed him. He nodded. "Every answer wrong. Do you have an excuse for this?"

"None, madame. Only apologies." He glanced up through his hair, excitement and laughter in his eyes.

"Failure requires correction," I reminded him, as I brought out a ruler—light, springy, no sharp corners—and sat down. "Lie across my knees." He did; damn, he was heavy. Next time we'd use the couch. "A strike for each wrong answer," I began. "Now: Five times ten?"

"Sixty-three," he sassed. I reproved him with a flat swat of the ruler. "Forty-eight?" he ventured. My next blow was harder, and I felt his erection grow against my thighs. "You require sterner measures," I said, pushing down his trousers and reaching between his thighs. "Next time, I'll correct you with my mouth. Five times ten."

"One thousand," he murmured and drew me to the floor, ripping a button off the suit in his eagerness to undress me. "Ten thousand, a million," until I stopped his mouth with my own.

THE SEXY SECRET:

1. Invest in a reliable, lightweight camera that you can easily use in the heat of action and that needs no mood-shattering adjustments.

2. Before you begin, talk about what to do with any recordings. You don't want past adventures returning to haunt you.

3. Film yourselves together with the camera on a tripod or bedside table. Fellatio or doggy-style intercourse is perfect if you aim to capture the up-close in-and-out. Woman on top records her charms best. Missionary position? It's comparatively modest on film.

4. Each partner can record themselves for the other's enjoyment. Lie back and film a masturbation session (flip around the camera's viewfinder so you can see whether you're correctly framed), complete with narration of your fantasies and thoughts as you touch yourself.

Night Thirty-Five
I'll Be Watching You

I handed him the oil, ordering him to drip it on his abdomen and thighs. I swirled my fingers in the lightly-scented sheen, drawing lazy lines up his penis and around his nipples. Then I poured a few drops into his palm and sat back on my heels.

"Show me what you do when you're alone at night," I demanded.

"Oh, I'm never alone. Not at night," he laughed. I straddled him and wrapped his fingers around his cock. Obediently he began to stroke himself, but still he smiled at me, refusing to take me seriously.

Suddenly I was furious. I darted across his bedroom and into his study, grabbing the video camera I knew he kept on his desk. I pinned him between my knees and raised the camera. "Now," I said. "You're going to show me everything." The camera between us seemed to lend me strength, and he sensed it. His oiled hand moved faster as the camera's tiny red light glared down at him.

THE SEXY SECRET:

1. The feet are quite sensitive, especially the toes, and attention to them is not only stimulating but deeply relaxing.

2. Make an occasion of his feet by washing them in a bowl of scented water. Afterward, dry them with a soft towel. Rub massage oil onto your hands and work your fingertips and knuckles deeply across his heels, arches, and toes.

3. Wipe the oil off his feet and take each toe between your lips, sucking softly and finishing with a kiss on its pad. The foot ceremony might wind him up for further action or unwind him into sleep. If the scene goes in the direction of true service, you might offer a pedicure to a female or male lover.

Night Thirty-Six
I Toe the Line

The finest thing about his apartment, I thought, was this bathtub, a sunken and vast black marble oval next to a ceiling-height window that revealed the entire pageant of the city at night. I raised one leg out of the bubbles, stroking him with my toes. "You have beautiful feet," he said, so I drew my toes a bit higher to tickle his penis.

"And yours, my love?" I asked, grabbing his foot. "Are they beautiful too?" Curiously, they were. Men's feet had always seemed like calloused, ugly things to me, but his were smooth and elegant, like the rest of him.

I licked his big toe, then darted my tongue between each toe in turn. He sighed in pleasure, so I nibbled the sole of his foot and then slowly sucked his toes as if each one was his erection. "You're serving me tonight," he observed languidly.

"That's because I want to," I replied. "I'm still in charge here, make no mistake."

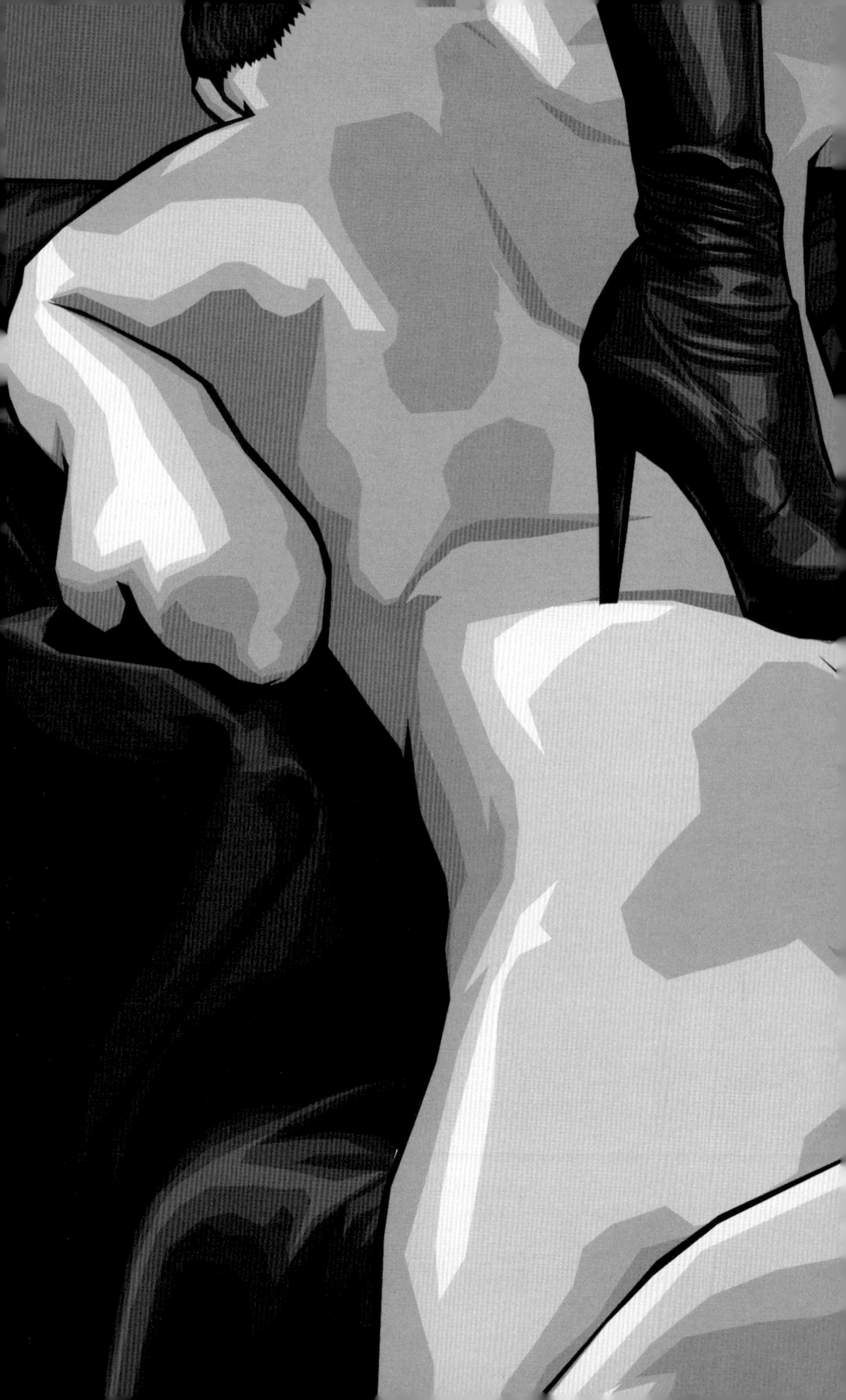

Night Thirty-Seven
The Stiletto Samba

    Boxes and shopping bags lined his hallway, each bearing the name of a famous shoe designer. I drifted among them, donning pair after pair of exquisite leather boots, studying his face to see which pleased him most.

    At last, I zipped up a pair that stopped just short of my bare hips. The heels were so lofty that I towered above him. "Those," he said. I turned so he could enjoy the view of my bottom cupped by the boot tops.

    "On your stomach," I commanded, and he compliantly rolled over. I stood next to the bed, holding the edge of the night table for balance, and lifted one heel to his rear. "Is this how my servant likes his massages, then?" I inquired. He didn't answer—merely pushed a small pillow beneath his hips for easier access. I drew the heel over the thick muscles of his back.

    "Watch me now," I breathed, and he turned to see me dip a finger into myself. I anointed one heel with my juices, then offered it to his lips. "Lick it clean," I whispered. He willingly slipped the heel between his lips and worked it with his tongue. Then he kissed my ankle and my knee, ascending slowly toward the prize at the juncture of my leather-sheathed thighs.

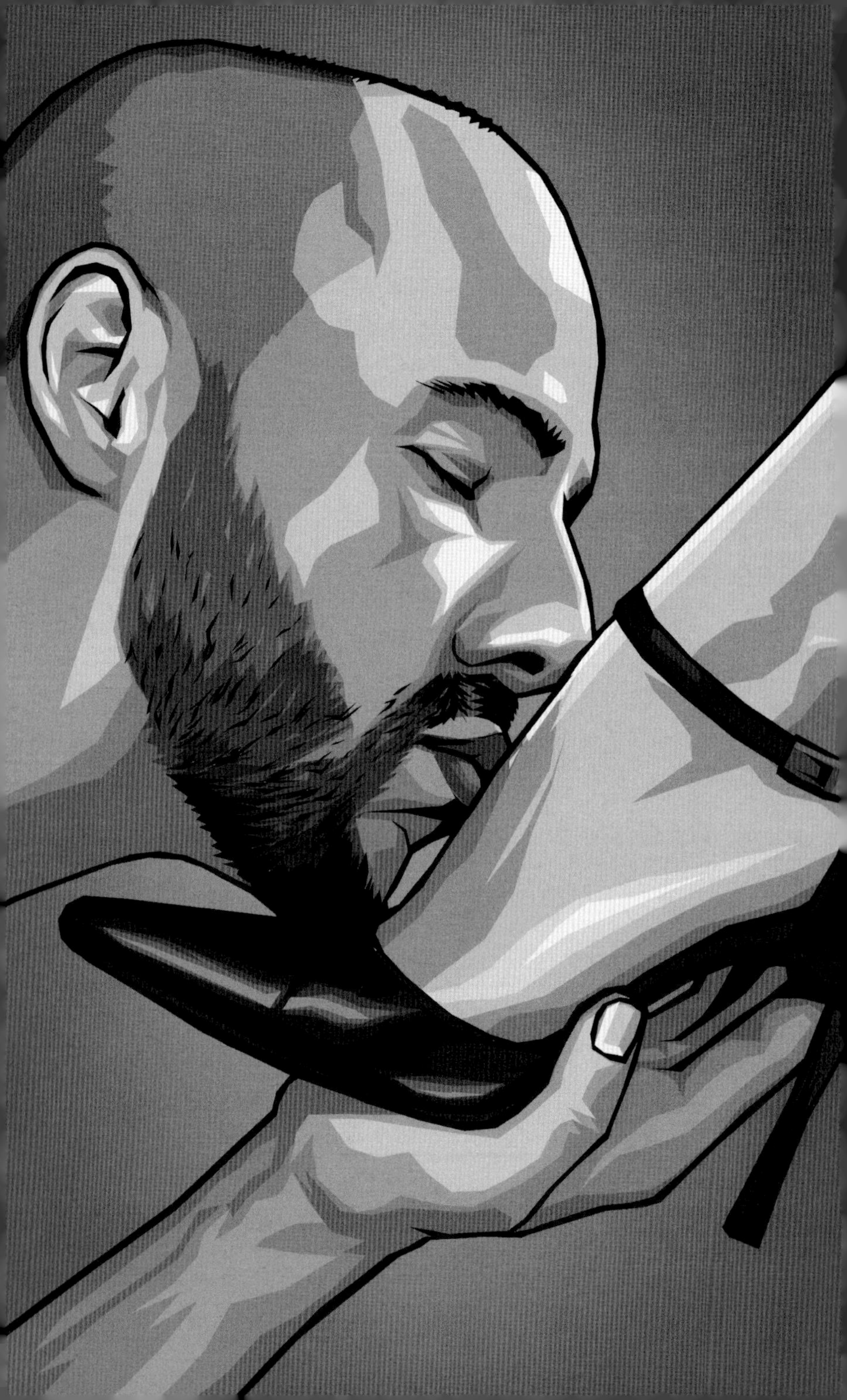

Night Thirty-Eight
Kitten in Heels

An exquisite pair of ankle-strapped pumps awaited me at home that evening. Maybe he believed the path to my heart ran right through my feet.

I slipped into them and out of my dress, then dialed him on video, crossing my ankles upon my desk and shifting the rest of my body out of frame. "They're incredible," I said, leaning in to finger the straps. "But I imagine they're for your pleasure, not mine." I couldn't see a thing on the screen—his study was completely dark, though his voice came through the speakers.

"Point the camera down a bit, darling, and cross your legs." He was topping from below tonight, but I complied. "Dangle one," he said. I slowly unbuckled one strap and pulled out my heel until the gleaming pump swung from my red-painted toes. "That's right," he said.

"What exactly are you doing over there in the dark?" I teased him. I slid my high-arched foot back into the shoe, then kicked it into the air, catching it and kissing its gold buckle. His breathing grew louder and seemed to catch in his throat. "Next time, we'll try this in public," he told me. "Good night, my love."

NIGHT THIRTY-NINE
The Wake-Up Call

He expertly caressed me as we lounged on his luxurious bed that night, but I feigned indifference. After so many nights as the avid student and demanding teacher, I wanted to try something different. I felt mischievous—I needed to tease him, to observe his frustration. "Tonight," I told him, "you face a new challenge: a completely uninterested woman. No matter what you do, you cannot excite me."

I rolled away into the pillows, feigning sleep, as he sighed with exasperation. Perhaps he'll masturbate, I thought. Perhaps he'll pretend to force himself on me. Delicious scenarios of being taken as I pretended to ignore him played out in my head. Instead he let me drift into sleep, untouched.

Toward morning my deep sleep began to melt into an arousing sensation. At first, I simply thought my strange, erotic dreams had just become a bit more realistic. As I stirred slightly, rousing, I realized his hands were on my thighs, slowly pulling me to the edge of the bed.

I pretended to doze, but his fingers probed insistently at me until he found the wetness he sought. Now he'll take me, I thought, but instead something thick, cold, and metallic entered me. *What in the world?*—I tried to sit up, but he held my hips firmly.

He was working me with a rounded crescent of shining steel. Inside I felt delicious pressure. Then he withdrew the thing and slid it across my clitoris. My body's warmth had heated it up, but it was still an unfamiliar sensation, so different from his hot flesh. "Cold, isn't it," he inquired softly, but I couldn't answer. "As cold as you. Can you resist it? Can you resist me?" I came hard around the unyielding steel shaft. No, I couldn't resist him. Ever.

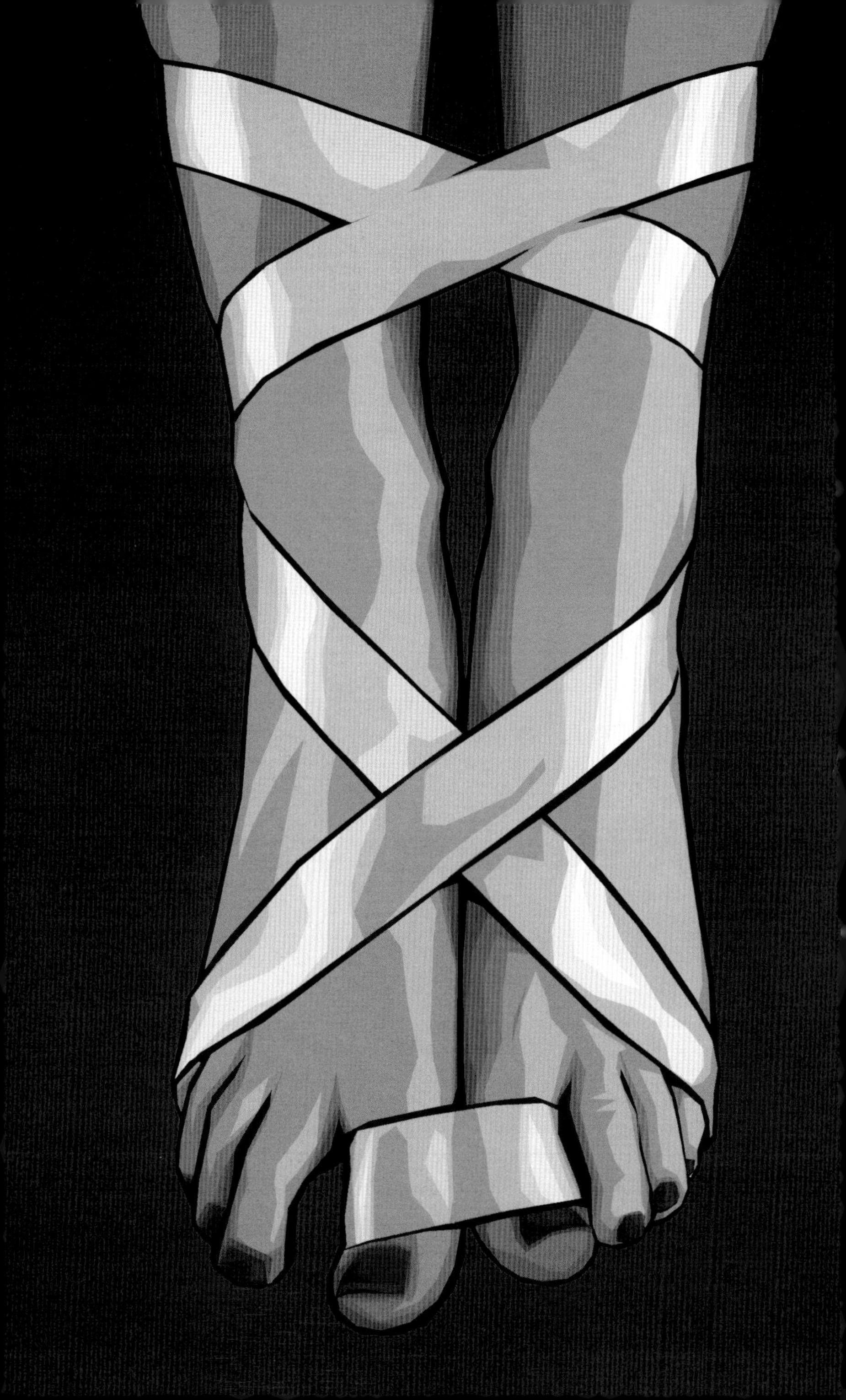

NIGHT FORTY
X Marks the Spot

One object in the playroom had as yet gone unused, and tonight, I was curious. I drifted naked toward the imposing frame, running my hands over it.

"Is madame intrigued?" he asked.

"I am," I admitted. How could I not be, facing an imposing X of black metal far taller me, with black metal cuffs dangling from each of its four ends.

"St. Andrew's cross," he whispered into the nape of my neck. "Crux decussata." I shivered. I pressed my pelvis to its juncture. It fit as if it had been made only for me. He stretched my arms over my head until I stood on tiptoe. Then I felt the cuffs close on my wrists.

"Not my ankles," I breathed. I wasn't ready to be that vulnerable, that helpless before him. Not yet.

"Shh, my love," he said, and I felt a whisper of silk winding and plaiting around my calves, my ankles, the soles of my feet. I looked down. He had bound me softly in silver ribbon. I was held by iron above, silk below.

He stroked me from shoulder to wrist, hips to feet, whispering obscenities in my ear, then entered me slowly. I pulled on my shackles and moaned, blissfully and completely martyred.

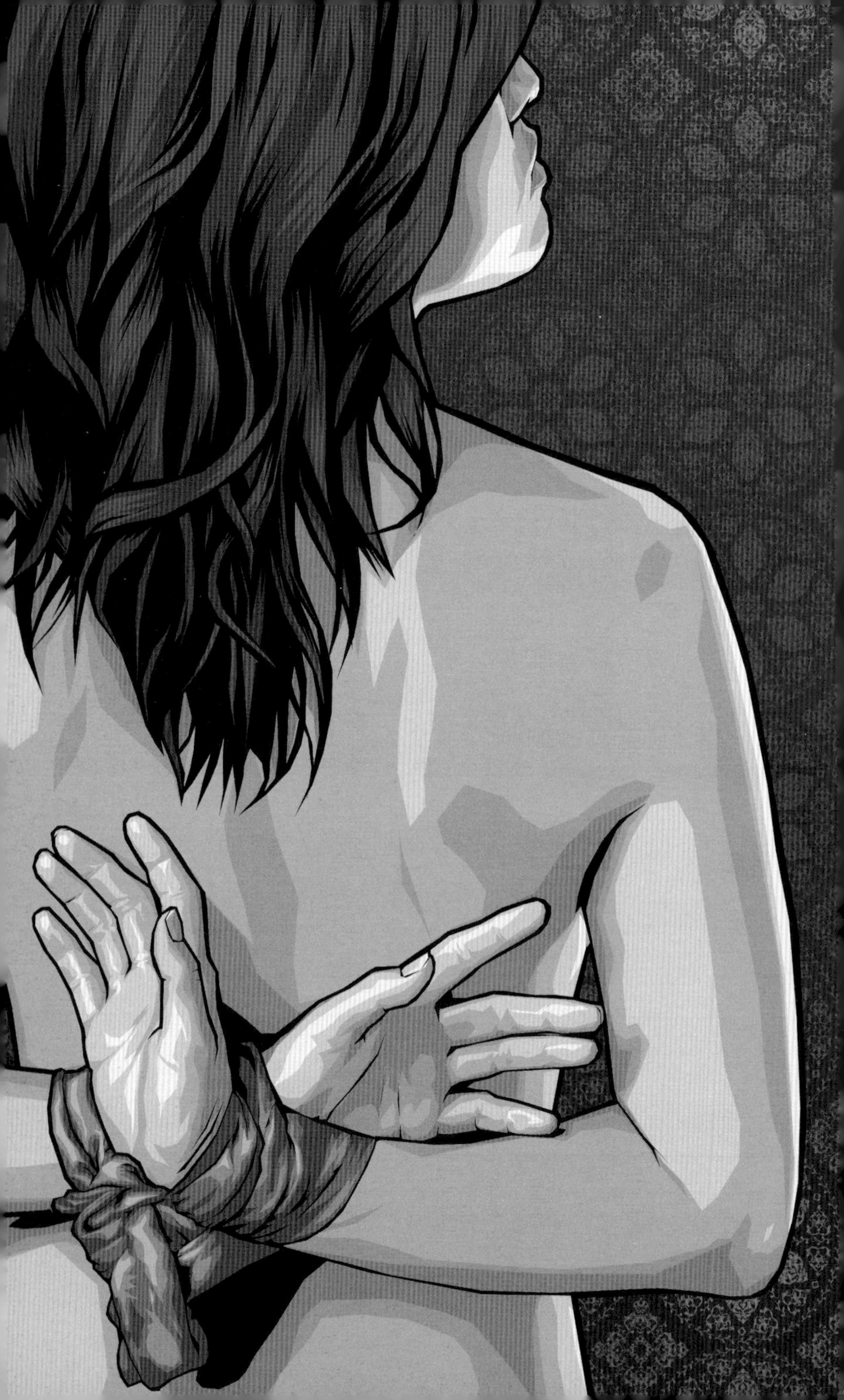

Night Forty-One
In a Bind

"You're not to enter the room before me," I scolded, distracted by the fascinating tangle arranged on the bed. My eye was drawn to a gorgeously dyed coil of red silk, nestled amidst dangerously rough-looking hemp and smooth, sleek white ropes.

"An experiment, my love. To serve you properly, I must know what pleases you." I felt again the tug of power between us. The lessons were mine to give, yet I knew myself to be a novice. I let him undress me and position me kneeling on the carpet.

He reached into the nest of rope, and drew out the crimson silk strands that had first caught my eye. I felt him wrap my wrists in the luxurious fabric, then bind my ankles. It felt... oddly comforting, as though I were safe in his embrace. He teased my body, running his hands over me, but prevented my attempts to wriggle into positions that might allow me some release.

"You, my love, have a hard time holding still. I may need to bind you with something rougher to discourage you from squirming. How would you like that?"

"Do I have a choice?" I asked, knowing full well the answer. He smiled, considering his next move.

THE SEXY SECRET:

1. Handcuffs are a bondage staple, but research before you buy. Police-issue metal cuffs are sharp and can hurt (which some might like). They're double-locking—you lock them on, tighten them, and lock them again to keep them in place. You can also seek out hinged professional cuffs. Both styles allow little arm movement. They're best for experienced cuffers and bottoms who enjoy challenging sensations.

2. Play cuffs from sex shops are padded, easy to unlock, and comfortable for lengthy restraint. They're made of leather, rubber, or vinyl, often in vivid colors.

3. Buy cuffs that come with two keys, and keep them nearby as you play.

Night Forty-Two
Traffic Stop

Studying his journal as he sat by my feet that night, I found that he'd clipped several photographs of arrest scenes. In each, a woman was bent over a car's hood or pressed against a wall as an impassive cop snapped cuffs on her wrists. Each woman's arms were pulled backward, her breasts raised. "Quite a portfolio," I murmured.

"Indeed," he replied. "I wish you'd do something awful so I could watch you get arrested."

I teased him with my toes. "I'd only do something awful if you were the responding officer."

"First I'd pull you out of your car," he replied. "I'd search you thoroughly."

"I'd resist," I answered. "You haven't even read me my rights yet."

"Then I'd force you onto the hood," he murmured. "If you struggled, I'd grip your legs between mine. Then I'd pull your arms back, hard, so I could stroke your breasts. I'd cross your wrists, snap on the cuffs, and ratchet them tightly so they bit into your skin. Then—"

"Bad, bad cop," I interrupted, drawing him up for a kiss. "No doughnut for you."

THE SEXY SECRET:

1. Bondage cuffs are a simple way to restrain your partner if you prefer to avoid knots and ties. Most are soft and include quick Velcro releases.

2. Start by binding only hands (or feet) if your partner's new to this kind of play. Full-body bondage on the first outing can panic a newbie, so give him free movement of hands or feet until he tells you he's ready for more restraint.

3. Bondage sets are delightful as well. They include the standard ankle/wrist cuffs, but some also feature attachments to collars (see Night Thirty), D-rings for chain attachments, and hefty buckles (the look of heavy hardware excites many people).

4. Never leave a bound person alone. Accidents can happen, and the person may need to safeword should their limbs become numb, or other problems arise.

Night Forty-Three
Stay a While

"Tonight," I said, buckling the leather collar around his neck, "we have a lesson in endurance. Hold still."

I pressed him against the wall, and slipped a pair of leather cuffs around his ankles, attaching their rings to short chains and clipping those to the hitching rings embedded in the wall. I bound his wrists with cuffs, too, then told him to bend his elbows so I could attach the wrist cuffs via light chains to the D-ring on his collar. Then, as a finishing touch, I blindfolded him with a silk scarf.

"What a sight you are, dear," I said, stroking his beautiful, elaborately restrained body. The feeling of power was intoxicating. "I'll return in half an hour," I told him. "If you've been a good boy and haven't broken free, you'll have your reward."

I walked to the door, opened it, and dramatically closed it. Then, barefoot, I crept back into the room. From the look on his face, it was clear he believed I'd left him alone. I settled back in a comfortable leather chair, hands plying lightly over my body, pleasuring myself at the sight of him so vulnerable, but forcing myself to stay silent, giving nothing away.

THE SEXY SECRET:

1. The anus is an erogenous zone for both men and women. Anal play stimulates a man's prostate gland and the base of a woman's clitoral nerves, and butt plugs are perfect toys to explore the territory below.

2. Any toy intended for anal play should have a flared base, to keep it from slipping inside. Some are rippled or beaded for extra sensation; others are equipped with vibrators. Whichever you try, lube them thoroughly and wash them afterward.

3. In pegging, a more intense form of anal play, the woman wears a harness-mounted dildo to treat her man to anal intercourse (see tips in Night Forty-Six). As always with back-door play, patience and restraint are key.

Night Forty-Four
Behind My Man

When he wasn't at home, I often explored the cabinets in the playroom. All this is mine to use, I reminded myself, pulling open a cabinet to find new toys.

Some looked like small, delicately sculpted chess pieces. Some were bigger and missile-shaped. Some were curved. Black, blue, metal, rubber. Such a collection. I caressed them, smiling as realization dawned.

When he entered the chamber that evening, freshly showered after his evening run, I ordered him to his knees by the bed. I kissed my way down his spine, then ran a finger lower. "I've found so many new toys for us," I whispered. "You've been holding out on me."

The first one I chose was a small, smooth plug, which I slicked with lube before teasing him with it. He submitted willingly, allowing me to glide it slowly into him. Once he was thoroughly erect, I drew the plug away. He looked over his shoulder to see me strapping on the harness I'd found. Its dildo curved upward, thick and red. I felt oddly powerful, stroking the shaft as a man would his erection.

"Spread your legs, darling," I commanded. "Farther. No, farther. Let's see how much you can take."

NIGHT FORTY-FIVE
The Back Passage

The following evening was comparatively civilized. We attended an intimate concert by a lovely string quartet, and then he took me to dinner at a rooftop restaurant. But as we stood to leave our table, he passed behind me and, quick as a flash, put his hand under my skirt and squeezed my bottom. Hard.

Ah, he's returning the favor, I thought later as we bathed together. He paid particular attention to my thighs and rear, caressing me with bath oil, then soaping me thoroughly. I pressed longingly toward his fingers, hoping he'd take me into orgasm, but he pulled them away from me each time I grew visibly excited. "Oh, it's not fair," I begged, but he merely smiled, drawing me out of the tub to wrap me in a huge towel and lead me into the bedroom.

I lay down on the bed, reaching for him. "Show me something new," I requested.

"I thought you'd never ask," he replied. He moved to the top of the bed, kneeling by my head. Suddenly he leaned forward and pulled my ankles up and back. He studied me in this awkward position, smiling at my uncertainty.

I felt the warm tip of his tongue between my buttocks and gasped. His finger entered me briefly, and then his tongue began a slow, maddening circle around my rearmost passage. He'd stop to dip in his tongue, then circle again. The feeling was completely new, and incredibly arousing. "More," I breathed.

And then he stopped, lowering my legs. "No more tonight," he said. Then he placed his fingers between my buttocks again "Tomorrow, my love, I plan to take you here. Study up, and prepare yourself."

THE SEXY SECRET:

1. The easiest position for anal intercourse is doggy-style or standing bent over. If the woman wants to control the depth of penetration, she can straddle him. In classic missionary, prop a pillow under her hips to reach her bottom easily.

2. Lube, lube, lube. The anus doesn't have natural lubrication as the vagina does. (And don't enter the vagina after the anus, to avoid any health risks.)

3. Take it easy. Some men prefer to orgasm via intercourse or oral sex first so they're not as eager for release; for women, be sure she is highly aroused. Then use a finger or a flared-base dildo to stimulate the sensitive opening, before attempting penetration.

4. Now enter her gradually, checking in to see if she's happy. Keep the thrusts shallow if she's nervous. Clitoral play will help her relax and reach orgasm.

NIGHT FORTY-SIX
The Journey Continues

That day I read everything I could find online about anal sex. The idea unnerved me, but I also remembered how I'd felt about our pain play before I'd begun to love it, and how blissful his soft mouth had felt on me last night.

Still I felt like a virgin in his bed that evening. "I don't know what to do," I confessed, and he smiled kindly. "Just lean over, love; put your bottom in the air."

He coated his index finger with lube and inserted it just inside me, softly circling my entrance. "Don't worry," he said. "I had a very thorough manicure today." I laughed and my body relaxed. Next he took a small dildo out of the bedside drawer and inserted it just a bit farther. "Breathe, darling," he said, and I did, and then I felt his erection there behind me.

In he went, one lubed inch at a time. I felt stretched, awkward, until he placed his fingers on my clitoris, stroking me in time with his increasingly deeper thrusts. I sighed and wriggled back onto him. Now this made sense; now this felt right. He worked faster, deeper, until he was completely inside me. "OK," I whispered into the bedspread. "This stays on our list."

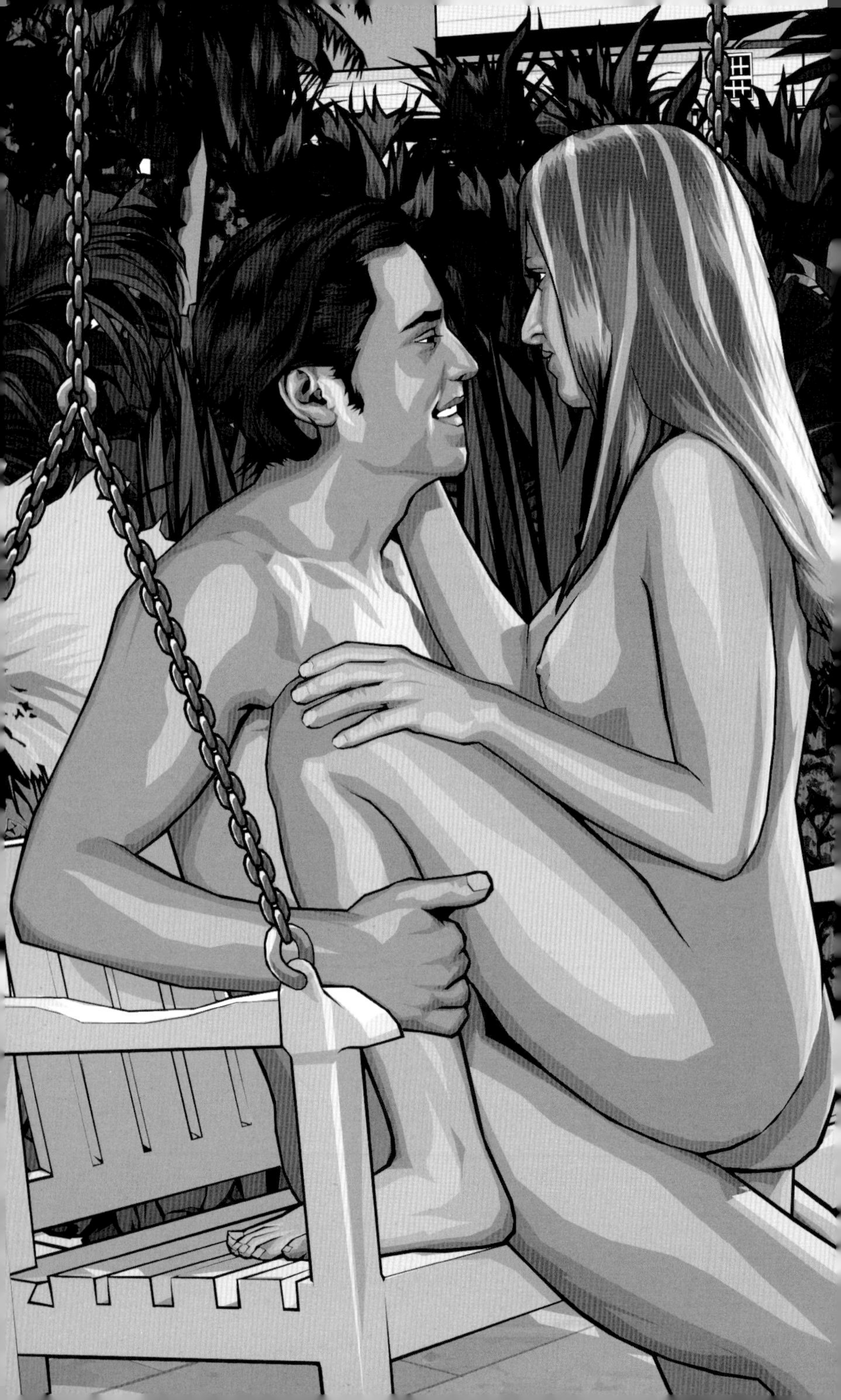

Night Forty-Seven
Face to Face

"Make an excuse," read the text message. "I need to see you... immediately." I was in an endless staff meeting, daydreaming about him. Apparently he was doing the same. I slipped out of the conference room, unreasonably elated.

"In here," he called when I entered his apartment. He wasn't in the playroom, but on the terrace instead. The afternoon sun was warm, and he sat back on the white chair, long and tan and beautiful.

"What's so urgent that it couldn't wait?" I inquired.

"A simple decision." He smiled. "I decided to make love to you all afternoon." He drew me to him, undressed me with leisurely fingers, and stroked me from my hair to my ankles. I relaxed, uncoiling beside him in the sunlight like a cat.

The afternoon unspooled slowly, neither of us in a hurry. He raised me onto his legs, allowing me to push against him as I wished. We paused for idling kisses and caresses. At last, as the sun set, he worked me with his hands and his favorite vibrator until I came in a long, shuddering wave, never moving my eyes from his.

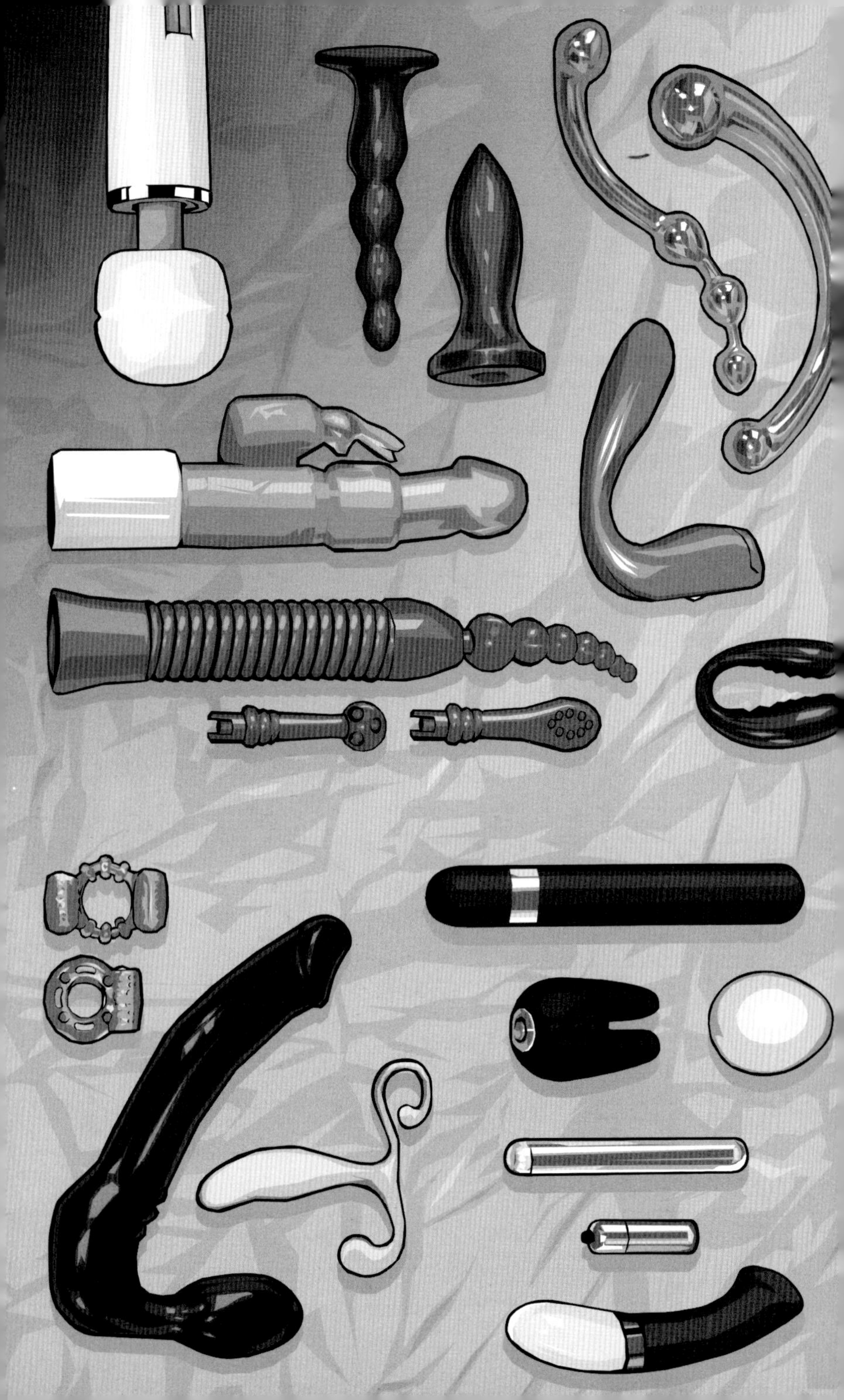

Night Forty-Eight
A Tantalizing Toybag

"Your collection is truly astonishing," I told him. I'd opened a cabinet door in the playroom to rummage through a treasure trove of... I wasn't sure what they all were. Glass cylinders with wires in rainbow hues. Antique assemblages of rubber and wire. Jade phalluses carved with exotic flora.

"I've been collecting since junior year abroad," he said. "I've brought them home from around the world." He drew forth a wooden object with a crank handle. "French, from 1890, and still effective." He spun its head against my nude bottom and I laughed.

He unsnapped a leather case. Nestled in its red plush lining were three silver balls on a silk cord. "Battery-operated ben wa, Burmese, from 1952." He glanced at me. "Would madame care to sample?" She would.

I reclined on the carpet as he inserted the slick spheres into me. They buzzed softly, each vibrating at a slightly different speed. "They sound like bees," he said, moving his hand between my legs as I grew wetter. I closed my eyes and held his wrist to direct his touch, dreaming of bees sipping at flowers in tropical gardens.

THE SEXY SECRET:

1. Ever heard of an elevator list? It's a fantasy list of people you'd jump, given a stalled elevator and a willing smile. But why elevators? Because they mix the thrill of public sex with the slightly weightless sensation of elevator travel itself.

2. If you want to try the up-and-down with your partner, scope out a quiet building and a time when you're unlikely to encounter anyone. Avoid your own office building—better to shock a stranger than your boss.

3. You might get caught anyway, so wear easy-adjusting clothes and get busy in a back corner so you're less visible. (Don't hit the emergency stop in a modern elevator unless blaring alarms get you off.)

Night Forty-Nine
Going Up

The following evening we drove for hours out of the city. I knew better than to ask him where we were headed. He'd tell me. In his own time. I laid my head against the window and drifted into lazy dreams.

I woke to find we'd arrived at a mountaintop hotel. It was a sprawling, beautiful Victorian, a riot of gables and towers whose giltwork glowed faintly in the moonlight. He led me across its porch by the hand and opened the stained-glass doors. But the grand reception desk was empty. No one was here.

"Closed for the season?" I whispered.

"No. Simply... reserved." He led me across the lobby, our steps soundless on the rich red carpet, to an ornate birdcage elevator. He worked its levers, and the strange contraption began to rise. Sleepily I stroked its scrollwork frame, then came wide awake as he flipped another lever and halted our ascent high above the lobby.

He raised my skirt, pressing me against the bars. "Are you certain no one's here?" I asked, as he wrapped my legs around his waist, entering and lifting me at the same time. "No." He laughed. Not certain at all, my love.

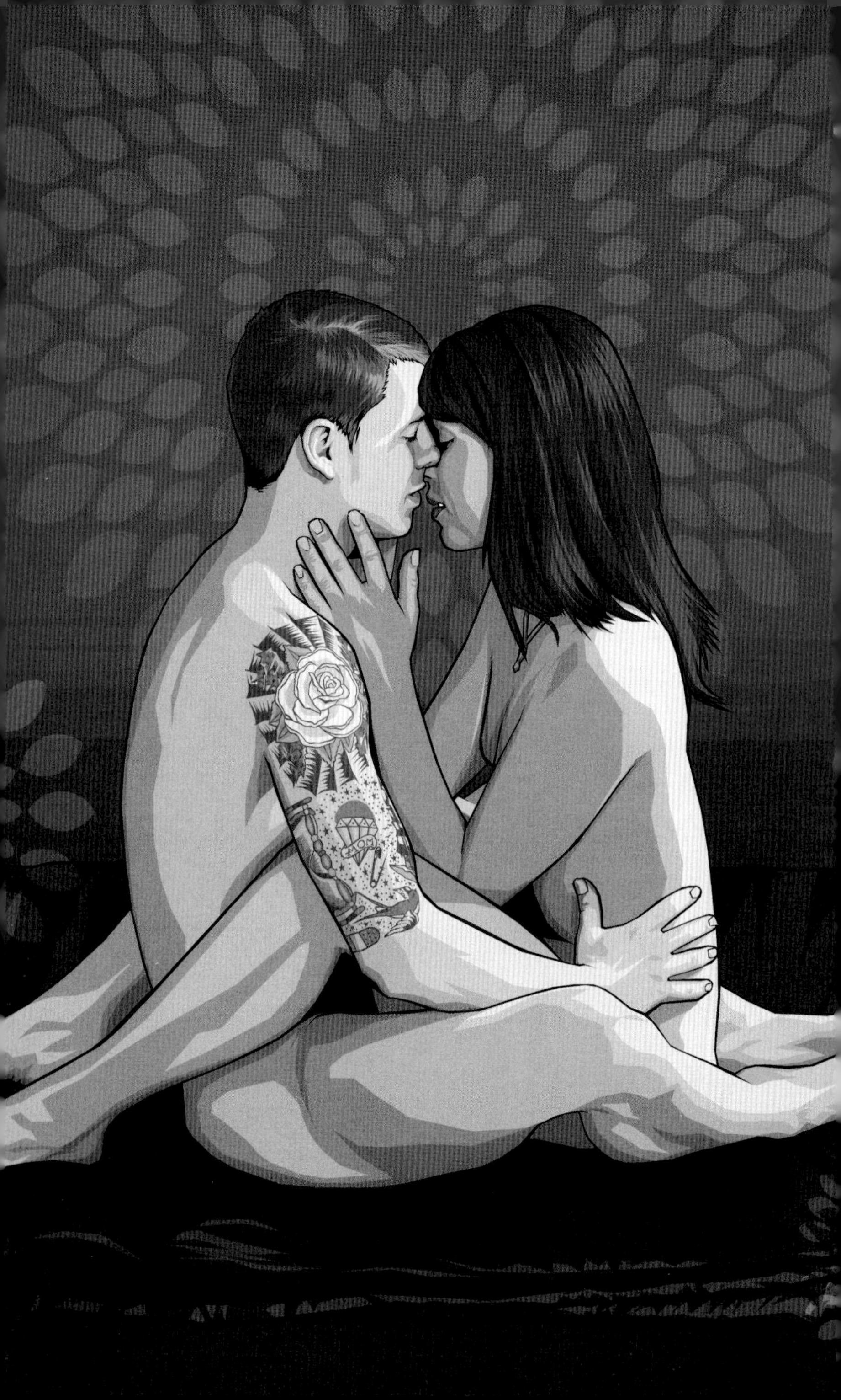
MOM

NIGHT FIFTY
Closing the Book

"I believe our studies are nearly complete," he mused, paging through the journal we'd filled with our drawings, our notes and fantasies and dreams. "Perhaps it's time we ended our lessons."

My heart fell. Were we done with each other, then? "There are still many blank pages," I pointed out softly.

He placed the journal on the floor and drew me toward himself, leaning his forehead against mine. "We don't need them anymore," he said.

He moved his lips up my neck. "As I told you at the beginning, the results may surprise you," he whispered into my ear. "They've surprised me as well, my love." His lips found mine. I knew then that our journey would continue, night after mysterious night, and that we'd write endless stories—this time together. It no longer mattered who was the student and who was the teacher. We would learn together, writing a never-ending story of love, lust, and experimentation. I closed my eyes, sought him with eager hands.

"Let the journey begin," I whispered.
"May it never end," he replied.

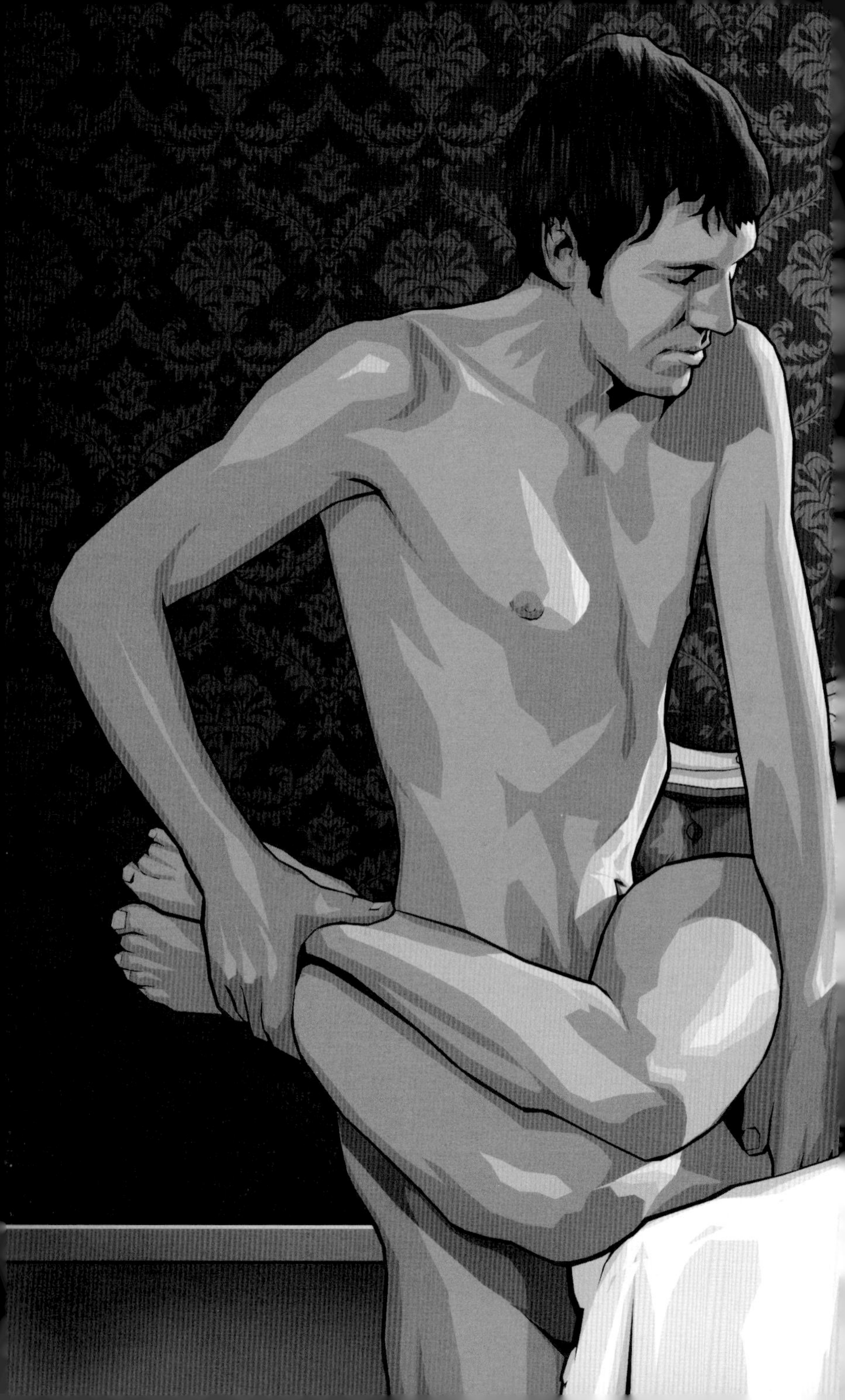

weldonowen

PRESIDENT, CEO Terry Newell
VP, PUBLISHER Roger Shaw
EXECUTIVE EDITOR Mariah Bear
CREATIVE DIRECTOR Kelly Booth
PRODUCTION DIRECTOR Chris Hemesath
PRODUCTION MANAGER Michelle Duggan

Weldon Owen would also like to thank
Ian Cannon and Bridget Fitzgerald for editorial help.
Katie Cavenee provided design assistance.

©2012 Weldon Owen Inc.
415 Jackson Street | San Francisco, CA 94111
www.wopublishing.com
All rights reserved, including the right of
reproduction in whole or in part in any form.

Weldon Owen is a division of
BONNIER

Library of Congress Control Number
on file with the publisher
ISBN 978-1-61628-536-4
10 9 8 7 6 5 4 3 2 1
2012 2013 2014
Printed in Singapore

TEXT Laura Elias
ILLUSTRATIONS Benjamin Wachenje

329

The End

. . . or is it?